KACIE HILTON

A Position of Trust

First edition

This book was professionally typeset on Reedsy.
Find out more at reedsy.com

Contents

Chapter One

If only it were legal to beat the shit out of someone when they betrayed you.

Isabella grabbed at the bottle of wine and poured herself another glass, stopping when it was close to spilling over. Casting another scowl at the picture she had of her husband on the desk, she took a generous swig. Then another.

And it didn't make her feel any better. She was just as angry as ever.

Her life was ruined. Her career was on the line. The man who had married her, claiming that he would love her through everything, had left her. Things were just getting worse and worse.

Would it ever stop?

If only that stupid girl hadn't blabbed to her parents about what was happening. Isabella thought she had scared the kid enough that she wouldn't say anything to anyone. It had worked in the past. So what was different about it now? Why did the brat decide now was a good time to tell her parents about how she was being disciplined? It wasn't like Isabella hit her hard. The other kids could handle it, so why couldn't she?

She had to go to court tomorrow to hear the verdict. But Isabella was sure that she knew what it would be. Guilty. Then she would be sentenced. If she was lucky, she could avoid jail time, but she wouldn't be able to go back to teaching, and she certainly wouldn't be able to work with kids again.

Teaching was her whole life. Isabella had never done anything else. She had been taught by people she admired on how to be the best. It was why she was the headteacher now. And it was all because some snotty little kid complained to her mummy and daddy about the way Isabella disciplined naughty children that she was in this position now.

She looked at her husband's picture again. At his smug smile that seemed to be mocking her. The bastard had lied to her. He said he would love her no matter what. But when it came out that Isabella had been physically abusing her students, he filed for divorce and left the house. How could he do that to her?

At least her fellow teachers were on her side. They told her that she did what she had to do, and nobody at the school was going to stand against her. The school board would, that much was certain, but her colleagues were with her. Isabella was grateful about that.

Ellen had told her many times, from when Isabella joined as a junior teacher all the way up to becoming headteacher, that she just needed to maintain her composure in public. Keep her head high and control her emotions. It will blow over eventually.

But, deep down, Isabella knew that it wasn't going to happen. She just listened to those she looked up to, and she was the one who had been caught. If she was petty, she would have said that this was not just her. Isabella wasn't the one who started it all. In fact, she was just one of several who had fallen in with a regime that had been going on since the school opened. She knew enough to blow it wide open and get more people into trouble.

Maybe she should do that. Then Isabella wouldn't feel so crap about being the only person getting charged with assaulting a student. She had to have learned the behaviour from somewhere, right? She should tell everyone where she learned it from. And it would be the truth this time.

None of it was going to bring her husband back, though. He was adamant about being nowhere near her, and he had taken the children as well. Isabella had no idea when she was going to see them again. Then again, they had said they didn't want to see her again.

That bitch screwed my career up. I'm going to make her pay.

Isabella realised that her glass was empty again, and she fumbled for the bottle. But her fingers knocked the bottle instead of grasping it, and it toppled onto the floor. She heard the sound of smashing glass as it hit the wooden floor, and felt the splash of the wine on her legs.

Snarling, Isabella snatched up the picture frame and threw it across the room. It knocked over a small table before bouncing onto the armchair and then onto the floor.

"Fucking bastard!" Isabella shouted, waving her empty glass in the air. "You said you loved me! Why wouldn't you stay? You fucker!"

She really needed another drink. So what if the teachers were coming into school in the morning to sort out the lesson preparation for the new term in a couple of weeks? The boarders had gone home for the summer holidays, so there were no children around. Just the security guard if he hadn't been sleeping on the job would see her should he deign to leave his warm bed. If anyone saw her drunk, who cared? Given the circumstances, it would be understandable.

Isabella wobbled a little as she stood up, the room tilting

abruptly before righting itself. Maybe she shouldn't get another bottle of wine. Two had been consumed already, and she had to go to court in the morning. Isabella didn't want to be caught weaving all over the road on the road to Ipswich; the journey followed a lot of winding roads. Not a good idea, and she needed to be somewhat presentable.

Didn't Ellen mention something about driving her? She was sure her friend had said she would get Isabel to court on time. Maybe she could have another glass or three if Ellen was going to be driving.

Thank God there were bedrooms upstairs. Some of the teachers lived at the school with those students who boarded during term time. The cleaning service always kept them pristine, and bedding was always available. She could take a shower and crawl into bed. If she was lucky, she would be sober enough in the morning go to court.

At least she wouldn't be seen until eleven-thirty. If it had been any earlier, Isabella knew she would be dead on her feet.

Making her way slowly towards the door, a flicker of something out the corner of her eye made Isabella stop. Turning carefully so the room didn't tip over again, she peered out into the darkness. She hadn't drawn the curtains, so beyond the windows there was just blackness. Being in the middle of nowhere was enough to give anyone the creeps, especially at this time of night.

Then it happened again. A flash of light. Isabella flinched as it hit her in the face and made her head throb. She covered her eyes, waiting for the dots of light to stop flashing. When she lowered her hands again, she saw the light flashing again. It was dancing around, almost like a signal.

The groundskeeper would have gone to sleep already, so he

wouldn't be walking around. And if that useless security guard was asleep...

Someone was out on the property.

What bastard was trespassing now?

Moving back to her desk, Isabella reached into the bottom drawer and retrieved her torch. Whoever had thought it was a good idea to come onto school property without permission was going to end up getting the rough side of her tongue. She couldn't believe that someone would stumble onto the school grounds at this time or night when the nearest village was more than a mile away.

They were going to regret catching her in her worst mood.

Unlocking the back patio windows, Isabella headed out onto the huge terrace. The delicately-created bushes stood tall on either side of her, towering over her and casting shadows while blocking out the moon. It was cooler than it had been during the day, and there was a brisk breeze that whipped around her. Isabella could feel goosebumps coming up on her arms.

Damn, she should have grabbed her jumper.

Gritting her teeth as the breeze seeped into her bones - whoever said that you felt warmer after drinking alcohol needed to be shot - Isabella turned on her torch and made her way down the steps, heading across the rugby field. The river was just beyond the field, separating the grounds from the farm on the other side. At this time of year, the ground underfoot was dry, but the forecast said there was going to be some rain during the night. Isabella hoped that she got inside before that happened; she was sure she could hear some rumbling overnight.

Or maybe it was the blood pounding in her ears. She was not sober enough to know what was really going on. Although she was sure someone was using the school as a shortcut. If she got her hands on the little bugger...

Reaching the edge of the river, Isabella cast her torch around, the tremors in her hand making everything wobble. The river was low, the banks shallow and devoid of anything except mud. The trickling of the water mixed with the rumbling noise in her head. Isabella shook her head and listened. Now she was beginning to wish she had stuck to one bottle instead of two.

It would be just her luck if she somehow slipped into the river and she couldn't get out. Even in her state, Isabella knew she wouldn't be able to get out of the water on her own.

The cracking of twigs had Isabella spinning around with a gasp, but there was nothing shown by her light. The riverbank showed no signs of life. She listened some more, and there was nothing.

She sagged, rubbing a hand to her head.

"Fuck, Issy, you're jumping at shadows now."

"Talking to yourself again, are you?"

Squealing, Isabella spun around, her light spinning, and then her foot rested on air. Her balance began to tilt rapidly to one sight, and she couldn't stop herself from toppling over. She screamed, scrabbling at the air as she fell. Then the ground hit her hard, sending Isabella into a spin. A moment later, the water closed around her.

Isabella got to the surface, gasping for air. Holy fuck, it was cold for the middle of August. And where the hell was her torch? Had she actually dropped it? She shifted onto her knees in the mud as she heard a chuckle above her.

"Now that makes me wish I had a camera."

Isabella recognised the voice. The shock of the water had pushed away the pounding in her head, and everything around her seemed to become crystal clear. She looked up and saw a dark shadow standing on the bank, shining a torch into her face. Isabella groaned and held up a hand.

"Could you not do that? It's hurting my eyes."

"Given the amount you've been drinking, I'm not surprised."

"What makes you think I've been drinking?"

She heard a sigh, as if that was a stupid thing to say.

"Isabella, it doesn't take a genius to know why you're here at this time of night."

"What do you expect? Danny's walked out on me, so I've got nothing to go home to."

"What about court? You can't go in your state."

"I'll be sober enough by then." Isabella was certainly feeling sober now, kneeling in the water. Thank God the river wasn't that deep. She held out a hand. "Could you help me out? I don't think I can do it myself."

"Sure."

The shadow moved, and then started slithering down the slope towards her. Isabella frowned.

"What are you doing? I thought you were going to help me out of here?"

"It'll be easier to do it when I'm down here as well. I can give you a bunk up."

"And that's a better idea?"

"Well, I can leave you to do it on your own, if you want."

Isabella growled.

"I'm not in the mood for this."

"Neither am I." Hands go under her shoulders. "By the way, I thought you getting charged with assault was not the right thing."

Isabella grunted.

"Thank you. At least I have you on my side."

"On the contrary, I think jail is too good for you."

"What?"

Suddenly, arms are around her in a vice-like grip, pinning her arms to her sides. Isabella wriggled, but she couldn't get out.

"If only they still had the death penalty. That poor girl who suffered because you weren't caught after the first time. Instead, you were allowed to continue. Just like the others."

Isabella was beginning to panic now. What the hell was going on here? Was this a bad dream? It had to be the alcohol talking in her head. She was expecting to wake up slumped over her desk. She had imagined all of this.

But the cold water swirling around her legs told her that this was very real.

"What...why are you doing this?" she tried to scream, but her voice was trembling too much. "What do you think you're doing?"

She jumped when breath tickled her ear, and a name was whispered. Isabella didn't need to remember when clarity took hold; she knew exactly who it was being mentioned.

It had been a long time since she had heard that name.

"That...that wasn't my fault! I didn't do anything with that!"

"You're not as good of a liar as you think you are, Isabella. You're a bully, and you're an accessory. You got away with it, but not anymore."

"But why are you doing this? What do you have to do with it?"

Isabella's head was pounding with booze, cold and fear, but the words sank in, and they hit her with strong clarity.

This couldn't be real. This had to be a bad joke.

"I don't think you'll be going to jail tomorrow, Isabella. But you're certainly going to hell."

Isabella screamed as she was suddenly hauled backwards, hitting the water with the grip around her body still firmly in place. It didn't bunch at all. Water poured into her mouth during her scream, and Isabella started coughing, her throat and chest heaving as they filled with water. She was desperate to breathe, but she couldn't. She was being held at the bottom of the shallow river.

Oh, God. This was how she was going to die.

Isabella was vaguely aware of being rolled onto her front, the stones and twigs on the river bed digging into her face and silt slipping past her frozen lips. And then she couldn't fight back the cold anymore.

She gave up trying to breathe.

* * *

Thursday 21st September 2000

I didn't think PB would be so brazen, but she did it. I heard her say to her minions that J shouldn't flaunt how good she is. That she needs to be taught a lesson. QB had told her to knock J down a few pegs.

That meant trying to drown her during our swimming lesson.

PB wouldn't dare do it with Mr D there. He's always liked J. One of the few decent teachers here. But Miss F was taking us. Some bullshit about Mr D being sick. He was fine that morning. I know that was a lie.

And she didn't do anything when PB put J under the water and held her there. Two more girls helped here. And they were laughing.

9

They were fucking laughing.

Miss F did nothing.

I tried my best. I jumped on PB and scratched her face. Later, I found out I had drawn blood. Nothing felt more satisfying than knowing that. And Miss F started screaming at me, telling me not to interfere. She wanted J to suffer.

It only stopped because Mum was getting something from home and heard the shouting. She's very scary when she's angry. Everyone scattered. She helped me get J out. Miss F tried to give me detention for drawing blood, but Mum said the girls who tried to drown J would be the ones in detention and PB should consider herself lucky J didn't die. She also screamed at Miss F for what she did. Dad told me later Mum would never do that in front of the students normally, but she had never seen something so horrific.

I hope Miss F gets fired. I saw the look on her face when J stopped moving under the water. She was smirking. I think she enjoyed it.

J was taken to the hospital to make sure she's okay. I hope she is. Her parents should take her out of here. Even with Mum as a witness, though, nothing will happen. Because the head will back up the bad guy. He always does. QB is in charge here, and nobody can touch her.

I hate her. I hate them all. Miss F is a bitch.

Someone should put her under the water and see how she likes it. I wish I could do that. Maybe when I'm old enough and strong enough, I'll watch the life in her eyes vanish before she drowns.

Then she'll know how J felt when stupid girls forced her under the water.

Chapter Two

Ellen turned into the road and her heart sank when she saw that Jake's car was outside the house. Shit, she had hoped to get back before he turned home. He must have left earlier than she thought, or she had gotten the time wrong.

He had better not have been looking in the wrong place. If he finds out...

She would just have to hope that her husband took her excuse for being out when she said that she was going to be home. What he didn't know couldn't hurt him.

This was one surprise she didn't want to reveal. Not just yet, anyway.

Going over in her head what she was going to say, Ellen pulled into her space in front of the garage and got out. Grabbing her passenger from the passenger seat, she used the security light to check that she looked presentable. Why did driving always make her skirt hike up several inches? It put so many creases into the fabric.

Ellen unlocked the front door and headed into the house, dropping her bag on the floor and kicking off her shoes.

"Hello?" She put her shoes on the rack beside her husband's and looked around. "Jake?"

"In here."

At least he didn't sound upset. Hopefully, he was too tired to ask where Ellen had been when she said she would be home. Or not question it too much. Ellen could lie, but only on face value. Even at her age, she had gotten basic lying down to an art, but keeping it up for long never worked. Jake knew that, which was why he said he could read Ellen like a book.

If he found out what she had been up to, it would spoil everything.

Heading through the kitchen, Ellen entered the dining room to find Jake sitting at the table with his laptop open. His thick-rimmed glasses were fixed firmly on his face as he frowned at the screen. Sighing, Ellen put her hands on his shoulders.

"You really need to get your prescription checked out, honey. It's going to make your eyes hurt even more."

"The prescription is fine," Jake responded grumpily, barely looking up from what he was reading. "I'm just not impressed with this new lesson plan one of my teachers gave me. It's not what I expect for someone who's teaching at GCSE level."

Ellen smiled. She had a feeling she knew which teacher her husband was talking about. He had been complaining about a certain woman who had started her position as geography teacher at the college. It was like she pushed the boundaries of what was the norm for the school. She kissed his head.

"Do you want a coffee? Or a glass of wine?"

"I think wine is preferable after what I've read." Jake slumped back in his chair, taking off his glasses to smile up at his wife. "Make it a large one, will you?"

Ellen laughed.

"You don't have large measures of wine, Jake."

"I've seen you drink it. Are you saying those are small measures?"

"Okay, point taken."

Ellen headed into the kitchen and picked out their favourite bottle from the wine rack. She wasn't planning on going out again tonight, so it shouldn't hurt. As she poured it out into two large glasses, her thoughts wandered to Isabella. When Ellen had left her earlier, her friend had been working herself into a frenzy because of her final court date. They would all be finding out tomorrow if Isabella was guilty or not, and then she would more than likely be sentenced in the near future. She had been pouring out a large glass for herself from the wine they kept in the cellar for special events.

Maybe she shouldn't have left her there on her own. She should have urged Isabella to go home and driven her to make sure she got through the front door. But Isabella had refused any help. She had wanted to wallow in her misery.

Ellen couldn't help if the woman wouldn't take it. And after tomorrow, should the verdict go the way nobody wanted, she wouldn't be able to help at all.

"Where did you go to?" Jake asked.

Ellen looked up to see Jake in the doorway, leaning on the doorframe. Even at the age of sixty-one, he had managed to keep himself in great shape, his white hair thick on his head with an immaculately trimmed beard. And that body of his was still firm after running for so many years. Ellen loved running her hands over those muscles.

When he let her. Jake had been so busy with things lately he was too tired to do anything else. Maybe tonight, after they had loosened up...

"I went to see Isabella with Lisa. Then I went over to her place" Ellen put the bottle to one side and handed him a glass. "We were discussing Isabella and the future of the school."

Jake sighed, taking a healthy sip of his drink.

"I don't know why you are still banding around her. She assaulted a student, and there is plenty of evidence that she did it to others. She needs to be held to what she did."

"But Isabella is a good teacher," Ellen protested. "She would never do that."

"Look, I know you've been friends with her for a long time..."

"Twenty-two years."

"However, there is a time when you have to realise that she's not a good person. She beat a student black and blue. The fact she's allowed on the school property is nothing short of remarkable. If it had been me, she would have been told to stay home and not go anywhere near the grounds."

Ellen didn't respond to that. This had been a point of contention between them. Jake was someone who believed if you had done something wrong you suffered the consequences. While Ellen believed that as well, she didn't like how Isabella had been sidelined. The courts were really going after her.

If they knew what Isabella was really like...

"So, who's going to be acting head in September?" Jake asked, tilting his head as he regarded his wife. "The kids from abroad are going to be arriving shortly, aren't they?"

"The first arrivals will be here next Friday. As for who is going to be acting head..." Ellen shrugged. "It's probably going to be David. He is the deputy head, after all."

"Good. He's a good guy. I can see things going well with him there."

"You would, seeing as you recommended him for the job."

Jake looked smug as he turned away.

"And I know he's going to do great as headteacher. I wouldn't be surprised if the board puts him in the position permanently."

Ellen didn't agree with that sentiment. Sure, David was a nice guy and he was very popular with both the students and parents, not to mention the other teachers, but he had only been there two years. He wasn't one of the old guard who had been there a long time. Why would he be looked at for headteacher instead of someone who had been at the school for years?

Shaking her head, Ellen pushed her thoughts aside. She was just being petty, that's all. Much as she wanted to be the head of the school she had spent teaching at since she left university, she knew her limitations. She was better in the classroom rather than being in charge of an entire school.

And she didn't want to make the same mistakes as Isabella. That was frightening enough to keep her away. If anyone accused her of abuse, Ellen knew that her life would be over.

Poor Isabella. She didn't deserve this.

"Do you think David will get the post permanently?" Ellen asked, following Jake back into the dining room.

"I'm sure of it. That man knows just what kids want. I don't think I've seen anyone more dedicated." Jake's expression shifted as he looked at her. "Except you, darling. You've made teaching your life."

Ellen smiled back in return. Jake always knew the right thing to say. She slipped an arm around his waist, drawing herself close.

"I can show you what else I'm dedicated to," she purred, slowly kissing his cheek. "It might require somewhere a bit more comfortable."

"God, I'm sorry, love," Jake groaned, gesturing at his laptop. "I need to get this done tonight."

"You can leave it for a couple of hours, can't you?"

"Ellen, you know what I'm like. If I leave it now, I'll never get back to it, and I need to prepare this for my meeting in the morning." Giving her a small smile, Jake kissed her nose. "Sorry. I'll try and finish up as soon as I can."

Ellen felt her mood deflate as her husband gave her a squeeze around the waist and sat back down again. He had been doing this a lot in recent years, more so since their son had finally left home to move to Cardiff. They were affectionate and there were plenty of kisses and cuddles, but it was like Jake's sex drive had disappeared. He kept making excuses not to be intimate with her beyond the occasional kiss, and it took forever to get his attention. Jake had said it was because he had a bigger role now he was the headmaster, but Ellen kept wondering if there was something wrong with her.

"Fine." Holding onto her glass, Ellen headed into the kitchen. "I'll go and have a bath. Then I'll go to bed. Naked."

She didn't wait for a response, going up the stairs. Just because they were over fifty shouldn't mean that their sex life should stop. Ellen liked to think that she still had a high sex drive. It's just a shame she couldn't share it with the man she had been with for over thirty years.

If she was lucky, she might be able to coax him later. But with the way things had been going lately, she might have had more chance of raising the Titanic.

* * *

Ellen pulled her car into the driveway of the school and headed along the one-way track towards the Gothic red-brick building that made up part of the school premises. The classrooms, sports hall and the sleeping quarters were built later on, but the main building was still standing, looking majestic in the morning sunshine.

This was her favourite place to be. Ever since Ellen had come for her interview at the tender age of twenty-four, she had known this was going to be her second home. Wolsey Prep was smack in the middle of the Suffolk countryside, surrounded by lush green fields and barely the sound of anything except the children when they were out playing, with the exception of the cows in the field across the road. There was something tranquil about the school, and it gave Ellen a sense of pride knowing that she had done so much for the place.

So many fond memories. More than the bad ones.

Nothing felt more satisfying than knowing nothing could take her away from her passion.

Pulling into the car park, Ellen stopped alongside a white BMW, noticing the deputy head David Barlow talking to Elizabeth. The receptionist was behaving like a giggly schoolgirl, playing with her hair while she smiled up at her companion.

Ellen shook her head with a smile. It had been clear when David came to work at Wolsey Prep that Elizabeth had a crush on him. She would watch him walk away, her eyes lightening up whenever he walked into the room. It was rather embarrassing to watch her fawn over a man who barely gave her any attention beyond being coworkers.

Although she could see the appeal. David was a rather good-looking man. Sure, he wasn't as tall as Jake, but he was made up of compact muscle. Brown-haired and blue-eyed, whenever he smiled he drew a lot of attention. And with his wire-rimmed glasses, there was a studious look about him that made him very attractive.

He had certainly made himself attractive to Elizabeth. Ellen wondered if the young woman was ever going to give up and accept that David would never look at her like that. She was setting herself up for rejection, and Elizabeth didn't take rejection well at all. Not if the last time she was rejected was anything to go by.

It was probably a good thing David was oblivious to it all, otherwise this could get messy.

Ellen got out of her car and slung her bag strap over her shoulder as she joined them.

"Morning, David. Elizabeth."

David turned, giving her that smile that reached his eyes and made them glint.

"Hey, Ellen. You're here early."

"I thought I'd get started on things before anyone else gets here." *And I don't want to stew over the fact my husband rejected me again.* "Looks like you two decided the same thing."

"The sooner we get everything set up, the more time we have to ourselves." David looked past Ellen towards the corner of the car park. "Although I don't think we're the first ones here."

"What?"

Ellen turned, and saw Isabella's car under the tree by the DT block. It was her regular spot, something about being able to drive away quickly without having to navigate everyone coming out of the front door. It didn't look like it had moved.

"Maybe she's come in to check a few things before she goes to court," Ellen suggested. "She would want to be sure it's all in order."

David frowned.

"We can do that. She needs to focus on saving her own skin."

"You don't honestly think that she did this, David? It's just the complaint of a vindictive parent."

"I don't know what happened, so I can't comment. But she's

18

so close to losing her livelihood, so she needs to put her focus elsewhere."

He was right. Isabella needed to get herself prepared for what was to come. Ellen could only hope that this went well. If it didn't...

"Shall we go in and find her?" Ellen headed towards the door. "I'm sure we can take over whatever she's doing."

And it would give her a chance to see if Isabella was drunk or not. It wouldn't surprise her if Isabella was passed out in one of the beds upstairs sleeping off a hangover. Ellen would have to drive her to court, if that was the case. She had said that she would do that if Isabella wasn't able to.

Not what she wanted to do this morning, and it wouldn't be a good look for Isabella's session in court.

It would be her luck to deal with that as well after last night.

Ellen fished out her keys and started to unlock the door, only to find that it was already unlocked. The stupid woman hadn't locked up after herself. How had the security guard not paid any attention? What was the point in paying for someone who didn't check that the school was locked up tight?

It was at times like this that Ellen was glad Wolsey Prep was in the middle of nowhere; nobody would be nicking anything.

Sighing, Ellen pushed open the door and strode into the lobby. Elizabeth and David followed her in, Elizabeth going behind the desk and frowning as she tilted her head to listen.

"Strange. The alarm isn't on."

"Isabella probably turned it off when she came in," David said as he got out his phone and checked the time. "You didn't think the alarm would be on if someone was here, did you?"

"I...well..."

Elizabeth's cheeks went a little pink, but Ellen ignored her embarrassment. She was going to have a few words with Isabella about what she was doing. If she had been here all night...

"Hey, guys!"

Ellen turned to see the young, lively figure of Leanne Durose coming into the lobby, her curly dark hair bouncing with her movements. How on earth did she manage to be so bright and bubbly at this time of the morning? Ellen was lucky that she could keep her head up without craving caffeine every five minutes.

"How are you so cheerful at this time of the morning?" Elizabeth asked as she straightened up from putting her bag away. "I swear you suck all the enthusiasm out of the room for yourself."

Leanne laughed.

"I'm just a morning person, that's all. So, what is the plan for today? Are we going to be keeping to our classrooms and get the upcoming term prepared?"

"That's pretty much it," Ellen said before David could answer. "And the sooner we do it, the sooner we can go home. I certainly want to make the most of seeing my husband before the students start returning."

David gave her a bemused look.

"You make it sound like you didn't just go to the Maldives with him."

"You mean back in July? That was a month ago." Ellen headed towards Isabella's office. "At this time of the morning, I'd do anything to be back there."

Even if she did spend it frustrated that a change of scenery didn't help Jake's libido. Sure, they had managed to have sex a couple of times, but Jake was exhausted afterwards. He kept his body in good shape, but Ellen didn't get to experience it up close as much as she wanted.

She needed to talk to him about his lack of interest. She loved him, and she didn't want them to drift apart because they weren't getting it together. Sure, sex didn't mean everything in a marriage, but she would prefer it to be spontaneous rather than Jake pencilling it in on his calendar.

"Where are you going?" David asked.

"I'm just going to let Isabella know that we're here. And make sure that she doesn't forget where she needs to be later."

If she was lucky, Isabella was sober and pretty much ready to go. She needed to be in court nice and early and give a good impression, or as best that she could before she heard the verdict. But given how the woman had been the night before, Ellen didn't think that was going to happen.

The door was unlocked, and Ellen went in. Isabella was on one of the armchairs, her back to the door. From her body language, she looked like she was asleep.

Then Ellen saw the mess on the floor. Glass from a bottle was scattered across the floor, and there was an empty glass on the desk. She could see the splash of wine on the wood. That was going to stain badly.

Shit. Isabella was drunk, and she had passed out.

"Oh, for fuck's sake, Isabella. Did you have to do this?" She strode over and put her bag on the desk. "I get that you want to get rid of what is going on, but did you have to go this far? And what's Danny's picture doing on the floor?" Ellen scooped up the picture frame from the floor, sighing when she saw the cracked glass. "Maybe we should put this elsewhere until things have died down. But I'm sure he'll be back. You two definitely need to talk."

Putting the frame on the desk, Ellen turned to Isabella. Her arms were on the chair arms, her legs slumped out in front of her. Her head was down, her dark hair falling about her face. It looked like she hadn't moved at all.

God, how much had she drunk? This was not going to be easy.

"Christ, Isabella. You're going to give the judge a bad impression. If he was going to give you a suspended sentence before, he certainly won't now." Ellen leaned over her and shook her by the shoulder. "Come on..."

That was when she realised that Isabella's clothes were wet. They were clammy, sticking to her body like a second skin. Ellen looked at her hand, and saw that her palm was glistening. What the hell was going on? Had Isabella doused herself in wine? But there was no smell coming from her, even as Ellen leaned in close to sniff her hair. She smelled like the bottom of a pond, though, and her hair looked very shiny.

Unease settling in, Ellen carefully eased Isabella's head up, pushing her hair away from her face as she rested her back against the cushions. And what she saw made her jump back with a strangled scream, her hands clamping over her mouth as she felt the shock hit her.

Isabella's skin was so white it was almost translucent. Her eyes were open, seeming to stare right through Ellen. There were stones embedded into her cheek, and her lips looked squished to one side. And her expression...she looked terrified.

Ellen's stomach heaved, and she tried to gulp in air. This couldn't be happening. Surely, she was seeing things.

But she wasn't. She was looking at a corpse. One that wouldn't stop staring at her.

Chapter Three

Ellen sat on the end of the terrace wall, a blanket wrapped around her shoulders. Although it was a very warm, sunny day, she felt really cold. She couldn't stop shivering, unable to stop seeing the look on Isabella's face.

She was dead. How was that possible? Ellen had seen her the evening before, and she had been alive and well. Isabella was angry, yes, and determined to get drunk. But not to this extent.

And getting drunk didn't explain why she was soaking wet. Had she staggered outside and fallen into the river? But if she had, how did she get back to the school? Surely, that couldn't possibly happen.

This couldn't be happening. Isabella had been under pressure with everything, and could be difficult at times, but she didn't deserve to die. Who would do something like this?

"Ellen?"

Ellen looked up. David was walking towards her, carrying a mug. He held it out to her.

"It's got plenty of sugar in it. I know you don't like sugar in your coffee..."

"I'm going to need as much as I can get," Ellen murmured. She took the steaming mug, trying not to drop it as her hands trembled. She gave David a small smile. "Thanks."

"The police...they've taken Isabella's body away." David ran a hand over his hair. "There's going to be an autopsy to see what happened, but I think we can all guess that she drowned."

"She drowned," Ellen repeated. She cupped her hands around the mug, not caring that it was burning her fingers. "But how did she get back up to the school? She couldn't have drowned and then come up on her own."

"I don't want to speculate, Ellen..."

"But even you agree that she couldn't have gotten back alone, David."

David hesitated.

"I know what we saw, but we can't jump to conclusions."

"How can we have a different conclusion, David?"

"I'm not a police officer, and trying to think about what could have happened is going to tie me up in knots." David settled on the wall beside her. "It's best to leave it to the police to find out what happened. It's not in my job description."

Ellen was about to snap at him for being so stupid when it was clear to everyone that Isabella had been murdered and someone had brought her body back into the school after drowning her in the river. But then she saw his pale face, and how he seemed to be trembling. His jaw was tight, and when she glanced down his hands were clenched onto the brick wall so hard his knuckles had gone white.

"David?"

"Sorry." David swallowed hard, lowering his head. "It's just...I've never seen a dead body before. I thought I wasn't the squeamish type, but seeing Isabella..."

Ellen could understand. She had never seen a dead body, either. She put a hand on his shoulder.

"Let's hope this is the only time we ever have to see that," she said quietly. "I know I'm going to be having nightmares about this for a while."

"It just...this feels so cold. If she was drowned..." David cast a glance towards the river and shuddered. "Why bring her body back into the school? Why not make it look like a suicide?"

"I thought you said you didn't want to think about it all."

"I know," David groaned and took off his glasses, burying his face in his hands. "I feel like everything's a complete mess in my head. That is not something anyone should have to see."

Maybe that was why someone had brought Isabella's body back into the house, Ellen wondered. To mess with their heads. But who was this focused at? Was there a secret message for a specific target?

Her head was going to hurt if she thought too much about this. And David looked close to breaking down himself. Ellen squeezed his arm.

"We're going to need to head back inside," she said. "The others are coming in soon, and we have to tell them what happened."

"Tell them what happened?" David looked like he was about to faint. "God, that's going to fall on my shoulders, isn't it? I have to tell everyone that Isabella's dead."

"Do you want me to do it?"

"No, I couldn't. You looked worse than I felt at the time."

"I don't mind," Ellen insisted, taking a sip at the coffee and making a face as she tasted the huge amount of sugar that had been dropped in. "Just let me have this, and I should be prepared for it."

David peered at her.

"You're stronger than I am, Ellen."

"I'm not feeling very strong right now. Isabella was my

friend, and I had to find her like that." Ellen forced herself to have more coffee, tugging the blanket around her. She wasn't shaking as much anymore, but she could still feel the chill. "Also, someone has to back you up while you get used to being acting head."

"Acting head?" David closed his eyes and shook his head. "I was preparing myself for it in the event something happened to Isabella, but this wasn't what I had in mind."

"I get that."

They didn't speak for a moment, Ellen's mind turning over what she saw. It felt like every time she tried to think of something else, images of Isabella giving her that blank dead stare came back. She couldn't focus properly. If this was what she was thinking, she couldn't begin to imagine how David felt.

Knowing that they couldn't put it off for any longer, Ellen got up, wobbling on her shaking legs. She turned to David.

"Shall we go inside now? The sooner we get this sorted, the sooner we can figure out what to do."

"Right. Yes." David pushed himself upright. "I don't see us getting anything done today. Not with the police treating this part of the school like a crime scene."

"You're thinking about work right now?"

"I need to think about something that isn't someone I've worked with staring like that woman from *The Ring*." David rubbed the back of his neck and flexed his fingers. "God, I didn't think I was that tense."

Ellen wanted to put her arms around him and give him a hug, but she didn't. David looked like he didn't want anyone to give him that sort of comfort. Instead, she gave him a nudge towards the patio doors.

Distraction was what they needed. If they didn't, it was just going to fall apart.

* * *

The atmosphere in the staffroom was at an all-time low. The police had taken the decision to tell the other teachers of Isabella's death out of their hands, telling the staff individually as they were brought aside for questioning. Two of the cleaners had needed to be taken to the matron to lie down, although the matron herself looked equally queasy.

While Ellen was annoyed that the police had taken that chance for her to tell everything what was going on, she was a little relieved that she hadn't needed to do it. How did you tell people that someone they worked with and liked had died and it was looking suspicious? Ellen had still been going over her speech in her head as she and David joined everyone in the staffroom, only to find that everyone already knew.

Sitting in the corner of the room, she looked around at everyone. Lewis and Henry, the two maths teachers, were by the window talking in low voices, while Leanne sat beside English teacher Kerry, neither of them looking at everyone or speaking. It was odd to see the normally loud and confident pair so muted. The science teachers, Dominic and Nicholas, were by the mini kitchen they had in the room, in the process of making tea, but Ellen was sure they had stewed the tea bags to within an inch of their lives already.

The other teachers looked like they were trying to find something to do, and they were failing. Ellen could guess what was going through their heads: who would kill Isabella? Why would she be left like that?

The only people Ellen could think of who would do this were

Amber Whitmore's parents. They had been furious when they found out what Isabella had done to their daughter, and the father had certainly threatened Isabella, promising to get his own back.

Would he actually go that far? It wouldn't be the first time someone at the school had been threatened, but it would be the first time a threat had been carried out.

"It feels like everyone's waiting for something to happen."

Ellen looked around at the plump grey-haired woman sitting beside her. She did look out of place with her brightly coloured clothes, especially given the situation. Ellen sighed.

"We're all in shock. I don't think anyone knows what we're supposed to do now."

"I can feel the tension in the air. Everyone's wound too tight." Lisa Shaw squirmed, shifting her legs so she could sit on her hands. "I feel like we should be doing something, and being inactive is not helping."

"There isn't anything we can do, Lisa. We just have to wait until the police come in and tell us to go home."

Ellen very much doubted that anyone wanted to do any work right now. Not in the same building as where a dead body had been. The school was old, and there were rumours of ghosts haunting the place, but they were just tales that people used to scare the new kids. Everyone could handle ghosts, but not a dead body.

At least nobody other than her and David had seen Isabella's face. The image of it was still in Ellen's mind, and she felt really cold, even with the blanket around her shoulders and the intense warmth of the room. It could have been a sauna for all she knew, and it felt like she was sitting in an ice box.

"I could do with a drink," Lisa muttered. "A big one as well."

"I might join you with that."

"Shall we go to your place, then? It's closer than mine, and I would like to get drunk as soon as possible."

Ellen frowned at her.

"How are you going to get home, then? I won't be in a state to drive you. Also, won't Nora get upset with that? She wasn't too happy with me the last time I saw her."

"Nora will understand once I tell her what's happened. She can't argue with that. And I'm sure you can persuade Jake to take me. He's at home, isn't he?" Lisa shrugged. "If not, I'll spend the night in one of the kids' rooms. No biggie."

"You do realise you're talking about something that will be occurring in twelve hours, right?" Ellen pointed out. "You can't be still drunk by then."

"Given the circumstances, I have no idea when I'll stop drinking. I can't cope with death."

Ellen couldn't blame her. Her oldest friend was not good with anything that was bad news. She had an attitude that was not dealing with no-nonsense bullshit, but when it came to news that could make her upset, she turned up the attitude a notch. She didn't like showing weakness, the only person she was willing enough to do that with was Ellen. Not even her girlfriends had been able to get past her defences. Ellen was the only one who knew how Lisa truly felt.

Besides, they kept each other's secrets. Lisa was the only one Ellen could trust with someone big.

Like that one when you were younger? The secret you never told enough else?

I don't want to think about that. Not a good idea.

"Heads up." Lisa nudged Ellen. "Miles is approaching you."

Ellen looked up, and barely suppressed a groan when she saw

29

the upper prep history teacher crossing the staffroom towards them. God, why did he have to join them now? Ellen had told him it wasn't a good idea to be around each other in mixed company. Why wouldn't he listen?

"I think I'll leave you to it," Lisa whispered as she got to her feet, dusting down her patchwork, garish skirt. "I don't want to eavesdrop on what you're talking about."

"Lisa..." Ellen shook her head. "You know..."

"I do know. And given the situation, I don't think anyone's going to care. At least you won't have to do it later." Lisa tossed her long ponytail over her shoulder. "I'll be in the art room when we're ready to go. Just let me know when you're leaving."

Ellen gritted her teeth. After the way Lisa just left her alone with the history teacher, she didn't think she wanted her friend to come back to her house. She stiffened as Miles sat next to her.

"Hey, Ellen." He gave her a tiny smile, looking shy. "How are you holding up?"

Ellen kept herself rigid as she tightened the blanket around her.

"I'll live," she said stiffly. Looking around and satisfied that none of the other teachers were close enough to overhear them, she turned to Miles. "I thought we agreed that we wouldn't interact with each other at school like this."

Miles winced. At least he had the decency to look chastised.

"I know, but...I heard you found...the body." He swallowed. "I just wanted to check on you. I know you're a tough woman, but..."

But I thought you might want someone's shoulder to lean on. Ellen could read him like a book; after all, she had known him for over twenty-five years. Looking at him now, there wasn't much different about him than when he joined the staff in his thirties. Now sixty-three, he was still good-looking, his ash-blond hair having receded until he had given up and shaved his head. It sharpened his good looks, in Ellen's opinion. Of course, he was a little softer in the belly, but that didn't take away from his appearance.

If she had met him before Jake, Ellen would certainly have been one of the ladies swooning over him.

Not really something to think about, given the circumstances.

"I'm fine," Ellen said in a clipped tone. "Just don't talk to me beyond this. I don't want anyone to overhear and assume that we're up to something."

"Well, they wouldn't be wrong," Miles murmured.

Ellen glared at him.

"Don't say things like that," she hissed. "Now buzz off and leave me alone."

"But we can talk later?" Miles insisted. "Will you do that for me, at least? You know there is a lot we have to discuss, and we're running out of time."

Ellen hated that he was right. They did need to talk, but now was not the time. Where they could be overheard? She was not that stupid. She swallowed.

"Okay, fine. I'll text you later and tell you when. But I've got more important things to worry about."

"Of course." Miles reached for her hand, but Ellen pulled it away. "Whatever you want, Ellen." He stood up, dusting himself down. "I'll wait for you to message me."

Ellen watched him walk away, trying not to look at how his trousers stretched over his backside. Wait, why was she looking there? She tore her gaze away with a growl. She was married. Staring at other men was not what she should be doing.

If your husband actually tended to your carnal thoughts, you wouldn't have to look at other guys in the first place. It's not your fault.

"Ellen?"

Ellen jumped. Leanne was standing over her, watching her with a frown. Not a normal expression to see on the usually easygoing, laidback musician.

"You okay?" Leanne tilted her head to one side. "You looked a bit tense there. Was Miles bothering you?"

"Oh, no, nothing like that," Ellen lied. She managed a smile. "You know what he's like. He likes to know all of the details, even at the discomfort of other people."

Leanne snorted.

"Are you sure he's not got a basement somewhere? I've heard of serial killer groupies..."

"Don't be morbid, Leanne. Miles is nothing like that." Ellen got to her feet. "I hope we can go home soon. Knowing that there was a dead body on the other side of this wall is making me uncomfortable."

"I get that." Leanne's expression softened to one of sympathy. "I can't begin to imagine how it feels to look a dead body in the eye."

"I thought I said not to be morbid."

That just had Ellen thinking about Isabella again. Until she moved her head, it had looked like she had passed out. The wet clothes could have been caused by her spilling a wine bottle. But those eyes...

Given how low the water was, she wouldn't be seen from the window for a while. It would have looked like an accident, that Isabella had stumbled away and fallen in. Getting her out and dragging her back to the school felt a lot more sinister.

Someone wanted her to be found. Unless she didn't drown, staggered back, and something else happened. Ellen had no idea. She didn't want to think about it.

"Was that there before?" Leanne asked.

"Hmm?"

The younger woman was looking over Ellen's shoulder. Ellen turned, trying to see what she was looking at. The fridge and counter where they made their tea and kept their lunches was there, and apart from a corkboard there was nothing else. But Leanne did look confused.

"What are you looking at?"

"There's something stuck on the fridge. I don't remember it being there when I came in this morning."

"Shit." Kerry got to her feet, her mouth dropping open. "You have got to be kidding me."

Ellen had no idea what was going on. What had gotten their attention?

Then she saw it. There was a picture on the fridge, which wasn't unusual; most of the teachers stuck pictures of their travels or families around the staffroom. Everyone did it. But this picture was different.

It was a school photograph of a girl, not older than eleven or twelve years old, giving one of those awkward smiles you give when posing for a photo. Her curly dark hair was cut short and neatly brushed, her dimples showing.

But it was the printed strip of paper that was stuck to the bottom of the picture that drew her attention more. Capitals, thick font, and accusatory.

YOU'RE NEXT.

"Where did that come from?" Kerry was staring at the photograph like she had seen a ghost. "I thought all of those were archived away."

"What does it mean?" Leanne looked from Kerry to Ellen. "Why would someone leave that here?"

Ellen felt even colder than before. She did not want to think about that right now. Striding over to the fridge, she tugged it off the door and ripped it up. Looking Kerry in the eye, she dropped them into the bin.

"It's nothing to be concerned about," she said briskly. "Just forget about it."

"Wasn't that...?" Leanne began, but Ellen cut her off.

"Someone's playing a joke on us, that's all. I wouldn't be surprised if one of the kids snuck in here and did that."

Leanne didn't look convinced.

"But if that's a threat, it could be evidence," she insisted.

"A threat? Against whom?"

"Well..."

Ellen scoffed and walked away.

"Don't be so paranoid, Leanne. It's just a prank someone's playing with a random photograph they found. Take no notice of it."

But even as she walked away, Ellen knew that Leanne didn't believe it at all. And, deep down, neither did Ellen.

Of all the pictures to print that threat, why did it have to be hers?

Chapter Four

"Do you believe it's just a prank?"

Ellen looked up. Kerry had come out of the school and was walking over to Ellen's car, her long, purposeful strides a little faster than normal. It didn't take much to guess that the woman was nervous, and Kerry was not the type to get rattled.

Sighing, Ellen gave up looking for her keys.

"Of course it's a prank. Someone snuck into the old files, found a photo at random, and stuck it up on the board when nobody was looking. It was probably Lewis and Henry who did it."

"I just asked them about it, and they said they had nothing to do with it. I'm inclined to believe them."

Ellen rolled her eyes.

"Those two can lie as easily as they can do sums in their heads without having to think. Who else would think it was funny?"

Kerry shoved her hands into her pockets, the breeze making her feathered red hair flutter around her face. The English teacher didn't look convinced. Ellen wasn't about to waste her time going over this. This was one of the maths teachers being idiots again. They had done it before, after all. Ellen wouldn't trust them as far as she could throw them.

Although she did want a word with them about what made

them choose that particular picture? Were they aware of something?

"I guess I'm getting paranoid," Kerry admitted. "After all, what happened with that girl..."

"Stop right there." Ellen held up a finger, which made the other woman fall into silence. "We're not going into it. What happened had nothing to do with us."

"But before that..."

"Don't start getting guilty over something that happened years ago, Kerry. You agreed with us at the time, and now you're beginning to sound like you're getting a conscience. Not the time for that."

Kerry bit her lip.

"It's just...after what happened with Isabella, and then seeing that..."

"It's just a coincidence. Lewis and Henry don't know what happened, and I'm not about to tell them." Ellen raised his eyebrows. "I hope you didn't."

"No, of course not. I couldn't get them to admit it, anyway."

"Then there's nothing else to talk about. Just go home, take a deep breath, and we'll be back in the morning once the police are gone."

Knowing that they would have to be back in twenty-four hours was a little annoying, but the police had been adamant that they had space to check the area for evidence. David had agreed, urging Ellen to head home, and they could start their work plans from home. Ellen didn't know why they couldn't do that in the first place.

And she certainly didn't want to go back into school now after what she saw.

"Well, just so you know," Kerry said as she glanced towards

the house, "Leanne has given the photograph you ripped to the police. She doesn't believe it's a prank."

"Leanne's been a paranoid idiot since she was a little girl. She was like that when we taught her." Ellen fumbled in her bag, finally grabbing onto her keys. "Just ignore her and focus on yourself. That's all you can do right now. I'm not interested in entertaining her stupid ideas about how we're being threatened."

"Even with the 'you're next' statement?"

"That's just to scare us. It's just blowing smoke up our arses." Ellen unlocked her car. "Nothing to do with us. Lewis and Henry will confess eventually, and then we can brush it aside."

"And if they don't?"

Ellen had a few ideas how to deal with that. She was good at making people talk and grovel if they had done something wrong. It was a talent of hers.

She was just getting into her car when she remembered that she was meant to be giving Lisa a lift. God, why did the art block have to be on the other side of the school? Sighing, Ellen turned back to Kerry.

"By the way, can you let Lisa know that I've gone home? She's gone to hide away in the art room and asked for a lift to my place."

Kerry groaned.

"Really? I have to go?"

"You're the one who runs marathons for a hobby, so it should be a breeze."

"Can't you just call her? That would be far easier."

"Kerry, how long have you worked here?" Ellen got out her phone and held it up to show the screen. "We can't get a signal out here. I would do better with two tins connected with a piece

37

of string."

It made it easier if the students had a phone - they couldn't use it while they were in lessons unless they were rolling around on the floor for that sweet spot - but it was also annoying if the teachers wanted to make a private phone call. Ellen had made a few complaints about that over the years, but nothing. This part of the county was pretty much a dead spot.

"Anyway, if she still wants to come over and get drunk, she can meet me there. I'll make sure that Jake is out of the way by the time she arrives."

"Okay, fine." Kerry didn't look happy. "Bitch."

Ellen ignored that and slammed her door shut. She was not going to listen to Kerry grumbling. She doubted that Kerry had a good word to say about anyone. How her husband put up with her, Ellen had no idea. It was a miracle that Kerry had actually gotten married, and to probably the most mild-mannered man Ellen had encountered. Complete opposites, and somehow it worked.

As Ellen made her way back down the drive and out onto the quiet main road, she found herself looking to the left a little too long. Towards a part of the road that had been firmly imprinted on her mind. The flashing lights, the shadows jumping out at her, and the screams. Even now, she could feel the jolt in her body when she realised what was going on, the pain in her body and the feeling of nausea.

So much time had passed, and yet she could still remember every detail like it had only happened yesterday. The look of horror that came up to envelop her...

A loud blaring noise made Ellen jump, and she stalled the car. Her heart racing, she looked behind her, only to see Dominic Holloway's car right behind her. The science teacher was gesturing at her, saying that she should be moving. God, that man was so impatient. How was he so popular with the kids when he was a dick as a person?

Resisting the urge to make a rude gesture in his direction, Ellen started the car again and pulled out, turning in the opposite direction to The Scene. Ellen had started calling it that since it occurred, knowing that she wouldn't be able to look at that place again.

God, remembering that night had just brought her mood down even more.

A few minutes later, she was back home. Jake's car hadn't moved, so Ellen just parked back where she had been only a few hours before. She felt a little resentful that Jake would allow everyone to work their lesson plans from home, while Isabella wanted everyone to come in. What was the point of that?

Isabella. Ellen felt her chest tighten. She could be a bitch at times, but she was one of those people you couldn't help but like. She didn't deserve what happened to her.

Trying not to remember how she found the body, Ellen headed into the house, absently dropping her bag onto the floor and her keys into the bowl on the dresser. She wondered which bottle of wine she was going to open. With the collection they had, there were plenty to choose from. Would Jake think this was a bit too much, seeing as she had had a glass the night before? Would he start asking if she had started drinking again?

Given what had happened today, this should be giving her a pass if she wanted to get drunk.

Ellen entered the kitchen and tapped a finger onto each bottle of wine, still wondering which one to choose. She had finally made her decision and was getting out the bottle when Jake appeared in the doorway. He did look pretty good wearing a polo shirt and jeans, his glasses perched on top of his head. Ellen wished that he would let her explore all of that to forget the morning, but she doubted that he would allow it. Scowling, she opened the cupboard and got out a glass.

"What are you doing back, Ellen?" Jake frowned at her. "Did you do something?"

"Why would you say that?"

"Because you said you wouldn't be back until this afternoon. It's not even midday, and you're not that fast at lesson plans."

Ellen took a deep breath. It was going to sound strange saying it.

"Isabella's dead."

"What?"

Ellen tried to take the top off the bottle, but her hands were trembling, and she almost toppled it over. She knocked the glass, and she saw it start to fall. Then Jake was there, snatching the glass out of the air before moving it towards the toaster.

"You're serious? Isabella's dead?"

"Yeah. Someone killed her." Ellen gave up trying to open the bottle and pushed it away as her throat threatened to close up. "I...I found her body. She's been...God, someone had drowned up, and then left her in her office like some fucking doll."

The composure she had held onto for a while now broke, and she couldn't stop the tears from falling. She was aware of Jake putting his arms around her, leaning her against his broad chest as he rubbed her back.

"God, I'm so sorry, Ellen," he whispered, gently rocking her. "I'm sorry."

Ellen clung onto him, sobbing into his chest. Everything just came out, and she wasn't able to stop it. David had made a comment that if she bottled things up too much, but given the circumstances, she hadn't wanted to show that she was freaking out. Someone had to maintain control of themselves. If David broke down - and, to his credit, he had coped really well despite looking rather green around the gills - then she would have to step in. Someone needed to keep everyone together.

She wasn't feeling very strong right now.

* * *

"Come with me, darling," Jake said quietly, moving her into the living room. "Let's get you sitting down."

Ellen didn't respond as Jake settled her on the sofa, tucking a blanket around her. Then he left the room for a moment, returning with a glass filled halfway with the wine she had been trying to open. It wasn't enough, but it would do.

"Don't you think about getting up to do anything," Jake ordered as he handed her the glass. "I'll look after everything. If you want me to go to town and get dinner from the chippie..."

"That sounds perfect." Ellen managed a smile. "Lisa will be over later, so we're going to need three meals."

"Fine."

Ellen saw the flicker on her husband's face, but she ignored it. Jake had his own opinions about Lisa, but she was a great friend, and Ellen wasn't about to change her mind. She had just had a shock, after all, so she should be allowed to have whoever she wanted around her.

A lancing pain shot through her head. Ellen grimaced and pressed her fingers to her forehead.

"What is it?"

"Just a headache. Pretty bad one."

Jake nodded, and got to his feet.

"I'll get the painkillers."

"There's a paracetamol box in my bag. If you could get that?" Ellen managed to look up and smile. "It saves you going all the way up to the bathroom."

Jake grunted and left the room. Ellen slumped against the cushions, massaging her head. She couldn't have Jake going upstairs to the bathroom. If he opened the cabinet and saw...

This was not the time to have another fight.

Jake returned a short while later, carrying a glass of water along with her handbag.

"There you go." He placed the bag in her lap and the water on the table. Then he crouched before her. "If you need to take painkillers, maybe you shouldn't drink. Shall I take the glass back?"

"Like hell you are," Ellen growled.

"Ellen..."

"No! I had to see a dead woman, someone I've known for years, and I would like to forget." Her fingers tightened around the glass as she anticipated Jake trying to take it off her. "I'm not giving this up."

Jake looked like he wanted to argue against it. Instead, he sighed and rubbed a hand over his face.

"I'm sorry you had to go through this. I didn't like Isabella, but she didn't deserve any of this."

Ellen scowled at him.

"You've been making your position about Isabella clear. I remember you objecting when she was promoted."

"Given what's happened during her time as a teacher, it's hardly surprising, is it?"

"What do you think happened that was her fault?"

Jake scoffed.

"Don't you remember the Christian family? What happened with their daughter? They named Isabella in their lawsuit. You were as well. Given the evidence at the time, it was pretty clear what happened."

Ellen groaned. He was bringing that up again? Seriously, the guy really needed to remind her of that time.

"That was twenty years ago, Jake. Isabella and I were hit with malicious claims, that's all."

"Malicious? Do you remember what I had to do to pay our portion of the lawsuit? How I went through embarrassment at work because of what you did?"

"I didn't do anything!" Ellen shouted. "They were malicious claims! What they accused us and the others of never happened! They were just pissed off because their daughter wasn't doing well. It was all made up."

Jake's eyes narrowed.

"Were they really, Ellen? Because it's not the first time..."

"Are you seriously going to start on that, Jake? Now, after what I've been through?" Ellen gestured at him with the glass, the wine sloshing around and almost spilling over. "We both know that was not true. That family was vindictive, and they got our money through lies and fake evidence. Nothing more. The fact you believe them shows how convincing they are at being liars. Isabella didn't take crap from that kid when she was acting out, and neither did I. And they call it abuse?"

Jake didn't say anything for a moment. He just stared at her to the point Ellen wanted to squirm. Why did he have to look at her like she was one of his students in trouble?

"You said Isabella drowned, right? Do you recall one of the instances in the lawsuit where that girl was held underwater during PE..."

43

"She almost drowned because she was not paying attention."

"She was the best swimmer in upper prep."

Ellen scoffed.

"Nonsense. Clara was the best swimmer in upper prep in all the time I've been there."

"She wasn't, and even Clara knows it. How is it that one of the best on the swimming team almost drowned on her own? Or have you forgotten her testimony?"

Ellen didn't want to hear anymore about this. It was making her headache worse. Putting a glass down, she fumbled in her bag for her painkillers. Snatching them out, she cracked two pills into her hand.

"I don't want to think about people drowning or supposedly drowning, okay? Not after what I saw."

Grabbing the glass of water, Ellen put the pills into her mouth and gulped them down, the water soothing her mouth but the residue from the pills feeling like they had gotten stuck in her throat and making her want to throw up. Taking a few deep breaths, Ellen put the glass on the table heavily.

"I'm not having a conversation about that Christian girl again. She was trouble, and she made our lives hell for me and my friends. Her parents were the same."

"Even though they were staff as well?" Jake shook his head. "You've never gotten over being replaced, have you?"

Replaced. Ellen never got replaced. And that wasn't what happened. She snatched up her wine glass again as Jake was reaching for it.

"Get the fuck away from me," she growled. "I want to be left alone."

Jake sighed and turned away with a shake of his head.

"You know what happened twenty years ago, Ellen. I told

you that it's not going to be left in the past."

Ellen ignored him, grabbing the TV remote and turning it on. Then, with a glance in her husband's direction as he sat down at the dining table, she cranked up the volume. Jake stiffened, but then he picked up his airpods and put them in. Moments later, he was tapping away at his laptop, effectively ignoring her.

God, there are some days when I hate him just as much as I love him.

He shouldn't have mentioned the Christian lawsuit. Not after seeing that girl's picture in the staffroom.

Hoping that Lisa didn't take long getting to her place, Ellen pulled the blanket up to her chin and sipped her wine as she watched a documentary. Was it about true crime or history? She wasn't really sure?

It was enough to distract her from Jake's words, and how the similarities between Isabella's death and that near-drowning were so close.

Chapter Five

Elizabeth stood at the door and watched as the last of the police cars left the drive and disappeared from sight. Thank God they were all gone now. It was a little nerve-wracking to be so close to a crime scene. Elizabeth didn't like it at all.

Things were not going to get back to normal for a while. The only time she had been close to a dead body was at her grandmother's funeral, and her body had been in a coffin. Isabella's...

It was hard to imagine how Isabella and David felt finding her body sprawled out in the office like that. Elizabeth knew if she had been the first one in there she would have been in hysterics. Her stomach churned at the thought.

Turning away from the drive, she wandered across the lobby towards the patio doors at the back. They were still open, a warm breeze coming in and tickling her skin. Elizabeth stepped outside, glad that she was in the shade. With the sun so high, at the right angle it could make the terrace feel like they were getting barbecued. There had been many concerts here, gazebos set up everywhere so people didn't end up getting heatstroke. A lot of good times.

This time of year was beautiful. Elizabeth remembered many summers sitting out on the terrace once the teachers who lived at the school during the term had gone to bed, having a cigarette and making the most of the quiet. There was something tranquil about the countryside, far different to her life in London. Her parents thought it would be good for her to go to Wolsey Prep and experience something different.

There was a real reason for her moving schools, but Elizabeth came to appreciate what her parents had tried to do. Now she loved the place, so much so that she had come back to work once she finished university. This part of the world was her home.

But it wasn't feeling like home right now. Despite the warm weather, there was definite chill in the air. It was like the murder had cast a shadow over everything. Elizabeth wrapped her arms around her middle and tried not to shiver. She should have gone home long ago, but she couldn't bring herself to do it. David might need her, after all.

She wandered along the back wall of the house, reaching the huge windows that looked into the headteacher's office. Isabella's body would have been moved already, and it had been cleared to use again, but even glancing towards the room was difficult. Elizabeth was half-expecting to see Isabella at the window, staring out at her.

She had overheard the police saying that Isabella was soaking wet, and the cause of death was more than likely drowning. Which meant someone had drowned her somewhere and then brought her back into her office. Who would do something that horrific? What was the killer trying to achieve?

I can't begin to imagine what goes through your head when you're being drowned.

Elizabeth turned and looked out towards the river at the bottom of the playing fields. That thing had been the bane of the school's existence, especially when Elizabeth had been there as a girl. Whenever it rained - and it rained a lot during the autumn and winter seasons - the river overflowed and finished halfway up the fields, making the football field and most of the hockey pitches inaccessible. It certainly made cross-country interesting when they went onto the land next to the school and picked their way through the water meadows while dodging pigs and cows that had been let out to graze. Elizabeth had always been under the impression that the farmer wasn't keen on letting the school use his land for a sporting event, and to get the kids to hurry along he let his animals loose to chase everyone on.

That certainly made for entertainment with the slower kids, and the losers who freaked out at the slightest thing that made life difficult for them. Elizabeth hadn't cared; she was one of those who was naturally good at running, so it was nothing to her.

Those days brought back a wave of nostalgia. There were times when she wished she could go back to those days. It beat waiting around wondering who killed someone who had taught her when she was a kid, and who had been damn good at her job. Isabella knew just what the students needed for motivation.

She was going to be missed.

Voices behind her had Elizabeth turning around. But there was no one there. It could have been a breeze, but the hairs on the back of Elizabeth's neck said that someone was around. With these damn big bushes, it was easy enough to stay out of sight.

"Hello?" She approached the nearest bush, giving it a wide berth so she could crane her head around. "Is someone there?"

The voices stopped, but there was nobody around. Not that

she could see, anyway. Elizabeth moved closer, quickening her pace to get around the bush. Nothing. Not even crunching footsteps that said someone was hurrying away.

Either someone was messing with her - there were teachers who liked to pretend they were still thirteen years old - or she was jumping at shadows.

Sighing, Elizabeth shook her head and started around the bush back to the school. The damn murder had gotten her so nervous that she was hearing things.

A figure standing on the grass as she came around the bush made Elizabeth jump, and she almost let out a scream. It took her a second to realise that it was David, watching her with a bemused expression.

"Elizabeth? What are you doing?"

"I..." Elizabeth pressed a hand to her chest. Her heart was still racing. "I thought I heard voices, and I thought someone was..."

David raised his eyebrows. Why did he have to be so attractive? Elizabeth could appreciate a good-looking guy, but David was something else. He was single, handsome and intelligent. And he had a sense of humour that could keep any woman's attention. He had certainly captured Elizabeth's attention ever since he walked into the lobby to say he had come for an interview. Elizabeth couldn't stop drooling over him, much like several of the younger teachers.

It was just a shame that he wouldn't do it on his own doorstep. David had made it clear that he wouldn't date another teacher, or anyone he worked with. Elizabeth had overheard him after one of the lower prep teaching assistants had openly flirted with him. That had put her mood down a little. It didn't stop her flirting with him, which David seemed to be receptive to,

49

but that was it.

She wasn't about to get any type of rejection from him. That would break her heart.

"What are you doing out here, anyway?" Elizabeth asked, adjusting her blouse. "I thought you were checking out the classrooms."

"Leanne wanted a word with me, so we were having a conversation."

So that was probably what Elizabeth had heard. A stirring of jealousy fluttered in her belly, and she shoved it away. Not the time for that.

"What about?"

David tilted his head to one side, regarding her thoughtfully. Elizabeth wished he wouldn't look at her like that; it made her feel aroused. This crush was too fucking annoying for its own good.

"She was concerned about something her son was going through, and she asked me for my advice."

As he spoke, Elizabeth saw a flicker of movement behind him, and caught sight of Leanne heading back into the school, glancing back at her before disappearing from sight.

"Oh. I see."

Elizabeth tried not to sound disappointed, but she apparently failed when she saw the look on David's face.

"Do you have something to say, Elizabeth?"

"What? Oh, no! Of course not!" Elizabeth cleared her throat, hoping that her flushed cheeks could be attributed to the warm weather. "I guess I spooked myself, hearing voices and not seeing anyone around. Given the circumstances..."

"I get it. We're all rather out of sorts with it."

At least he wasn't looking pale anymore. The colour had come back, but there was something in his eyes that gave Elizabeth pause. She couldn't begin to imagine how he felt right now after finding a dead body. Ellen had to be in pieces as well; the woman was so strong, but even something like what she went through had to have shaken her resolve.

"Do...do you need me for anything else?" Elizabeth approached him, putting on what she hoped was a bright smile. "Or shall I head home now?"

"I thought you went home ages ago."

"I had to make sure the police were gone first. Someone had to make sure they didn't do anything stupid."

David grunted.

"Well, I'm planning to head home shortly, so there's not much point in hanging around. The groundskeepers can lock up after us."

"Are we coming in tomorrow morning?"

"The police say that we should carry on as normal, and I intend to do that. We have students coming in and a term to prepare for."

"We could just do it at home," Elizabeth suggested, at which David shrugged.

"We might be able to, but there are things we have to do in the school. The classrooms are in another part of the school, anyway, so they won't be anywhere near the office."

"If you're a teacher," Elizabeth reminded him. "But I won't be. I will feel like I'm expecting a ghost to appear."

David's mouth twitched.

"You're seriously not afraid of ghosts, are you, Elizabeth?"

"Normally, I'm not." Elizabeth folded her arms, hunching over as the warm breeze turned into a chill that she couldn't shift. "But given how soon after Isabella's death it's been...I guess I'm feeling a little jumpy."

Even now, she refused to look over at the office window. She really didn't want to find out that ghosts really did exist and Isabella was actually there.

"You have nothing to worry about."

"Are you going to be in there? You're the acting head now, aren't you?"

"On occasion. I've got my own work to deal with, so I'm not going to spend all day in there. But I'm not scared."

Elizabeth snorted.

"I don't believe that."

"It's not ghosts I'm scared of. It's the real things that are lurking in the shadows that frighten me." David looked around, something flickering on his face before it was gone. "And there are a lot of very real things to be scared of."

"Like what?"

All Elizabeth got in return was that smile that made her heart flutter, and David turned away.

"You head home, Elizabeth. We all need to take a deep breath and distract ourselves with something. But I expect you to be professional and get back to work tomorrow. We can let things slide because of this."

"Yes, sir," Elizabeth murmured. She hurried after him and into the lobby. "Although it does make us feel a little insensitive. After all..."

"My mum always said we need to keep going, even when something horrible happens. If we stop to think, it's going to come crashing down and procrastination becomes our best friend. With our profession, we can't afford to slow down just yet."

Elizabeth could agree with what he said, but she didn't think anyone else would. It couldn't hurt to leave it for a few days, could it? Then again, with the overseas students coming in next week...

She was glad that she wasn't the headteacher; she didn't think she would be able to cope. Isabella had shown the hard way how tough it was being the head of a school.

* * *

"There we go," Lisa said as she filled her glass up. "That's much better now."

Ellen managed a smile as she raised her own glass.

"I'm glad you're here, Lisa."

"Same." Lisa gestured towards the dining room. "Although Mr Grumpy over there isn't so keen about it."

Ellen barely gave the back of her husband's head a glance, Jake barely reacting. His airpods were pretty good if they were blocking out their conversation. Good thing, too; Ellen wasn't willing to converse with the man. She was still pissed off with him about his comments earlier.

"Ignore him. He's stressed about the start of term."

It was better not to have Lisa and Jake interact beyond the basic niceties. Lisa was aware of Jake's dislike for her, so she did tend to goad him, especially if she had had a drink.

Perhaps agreeing to have her friend over was a bad idea, especially after she and Jake had exchanged words. But Ellen wasn't about to change anything to soothe her husband's mood. He barely reacted, as it was, listening to whatever was blasting through his airpods and working away. When he was busy, he shut everything else out.

Useful, but also annoying when she could hear the tinny

sound of the awful crap he listened to.

"Why are you still married to him, Ellen?" Lisa asked. "He's a dick."

"He's only a dick to you, Lisa. And we work well together."

"Oh, really?"

Ellen rolled her eyes.

"I know you hate men, but you don't need to preach it at me in the hopes I'll agree. Jake is my husband."

"But you don't love him, do you?"

"What?" Ellen looked over at Jake, hoping that the blaring music was loud enough that he couldn't hear them. Even then, she lowered her voice. "Why on earth would you say that when he's right there?"

"Oh, stop fussing. He can't hear me." Lisa waved her hand around. "In any case, you know I'm right."

There were times when Ellen regretted having Lisa as a confidant. She glared at her friend.

"You really need to stop having loose lips. You're going to get people into trouble."

Lisa shrugged.

"No more than usual."

Ellen didn't want to talk about Jake. She was still seething from his comments about Isabella and reminding her what happened twenty years ago. Or what he perceived happened twenty years ago. Things had been greatly exaggerated, and Ellen had gotten caught up in the maelstrom.

She had never been so relieved to see the back of that family.

"Who do you think did this?" Lisa asked, taking a generous sip of her wine.

"I have no idea. Whoever it is has to be cold as ice to drown her and then drag her back into the house. I mean, why not leave her in the river? Given how low the water line was, she wouldn't have been found immediately."

"Maybe the killer wanted her to be found quickly?"

"For what reason?" Ellen pushed.

"I don't know! I'm not a mind reader." Lisa pointed at Ellen. "You know this is the work of a man, don't you? It has to be."

Here it came. More ranting about men. Ellen knew Lisa's past and understood why she hated men, but it did go to another level. She shook her head.

"It could be a woman. Or it could be more than one person."

"Well, a man is certainly involved," Lisa declared, belching as she took another gulp of her wine. Ellen had no idea how her friend could knock wine back like it was water. "And my money is on Lewis Whitmore."

Ellen frowned.

"Amber Whitmore's father?"

"He threatened Isabella, didn't he? He said he would make sure she ended up in hell for laying a hand on his kid."

"That man has always had a temper." Ellen didn't realise that she was waving her glass around until the wine sloshed onto her hand. Groaning, she reached for the tissue box, putting her glass down to mop herself up. "If he didn't have the money to easily pay the tuition fees, he wouldn't be here at all."

"Well, he was furious. Isabella said she was nervous of him at court, and there were court officers all around the room."

Ellen thought about it as she cleaned herself, glad that she didn't get more than a couple of drops onto her blanket. It was a possibility. Lewis Whitmore was a doctor, and a brilliant one at that, but he was also quick to anger. Some people would call it justifiable, but Ellen thought it was too much. She had had many upset parents come into the school to complain about the treatment of their kids, but they could be smoothed over. It was always a misunderstanding. But Whitmore refused to listen to reason. He was adamant that Isabella paid for what she did.

He was the reason Isabella's life was being ruined. Him and that little girl. They exaggerated her detentions. Ellen wouldn't be surprised if they exaggerated the injuries as well. She had been at court for one of those days, and she saw the pictures. It wouldn't take much to manipulate and photoshop the pictures.

But that's not what happened, is it?

"I'm sure the police have already spoken to him by now," Ellen said as she sat back, picking up her glass again. "Although I'm sure he has an alibi that's rock-solid."

Lisa snorted.

"Even the most solid of alibis can be broken. They'll catch him."

She was so certain that it was Whitmore. Part of Ellen could see it happening. But, at the same time, she couldn't see Whitmore doing that. While he did have a temper, he never threw his fists. Sure, he threw things around, but he didn't hit anyone. Ellen could see him as the type who hit someone and immediately apologised afterwards.

Besides, this seemed sadistic, and Whitmore didn't strike her as that. Hot-tempered, yes, but not sadistic enough to drown someone and drag them elsewhere.

The bleeping of her phone had Ellen looking over. She had left it facedown on the table, not wanting to look at it and thinking she was getting a call from Isabella, just like any other night. Isabella was always calling her, mostly for advice but also just to talk. Knowing that the younger woman still looked up to her had made Ellen feel proud.

She mentally shook herself. Now this was stupid. It wasn't Isabella, and you don't believe in ghosts. Ellen picked up her phone and opened up the message.

We still need to talk. Meet me please. I want to see you. x

She groaned. God, why now?

"What is it?" Lisa frowned at her. "That was a pretty big groan."

"It's Miles. Again." Ellen showed her friend the message. "He's still trying to contact me."

"What? I thought you said..."

"I did. He's not getting the message." Ellen hesitated. "What do I say? I don't want him to think anything's happening."

Lisa scoffed.

"I think you're past that point. You need to tell him where to go, Ellen, otherwise he's never going to get the message."

"He's not gotten it so far before."

She did have a point. And while telling him by text would be better, this needed to be done face to face. Miles needed to be told, and Ellen would have to look him in the eye.

She could do it with the kids, so why couldn't she do it with someone she has known for years.

"Okay, fine." Her fingers moved across the touchpad. "Let's get this done."

Fine. Tell me when.

The response came back very quickly. Miles must have been staring at his screen waiting for her reply.

DT workshop. Before everyone gets there. x

Ellen frowned.

Why then?

Easier and more convenient. Unless you want to meet me in the night...;) x

God, why did he have to do this? Lisa snorted as she looked over my shoulder.

"Honestly, he can be such a creep."

"He's not a creep, Lisa. He's decent enough."

"Enough that he's pestering you?"

She had a point. Ellen concentrated on her response.

Fine. Seven tomorrow morning. You'd better have the keys. I don't want anyone to see us.

Thanks Ellen. You won't regret this x

Wishing that he wouldn't put kisses on the end of his texts, Ellen put her phone aside. She had a feeling that she was going to regret this.

Chapter Six

Miles could feel his skin tingling as he pulled up outside the design technology workshop. At this time of night, the groundskeepers would be fast asleep, and they were on the far side of the grounds. The security guard was shit as his job as well. Nobody would be disturbing them.

He couldn't wait to see Ellen. Being in her presence and not being able to touch her as he wanted made him feel like he was crawling out of her skin. She had the ability to make him weak at the knees, and Miles never thought that would happen to him. Then he had come to Wolsey Prep and met Ellen, and things had changed.

It was so difficult to keep away when she was married, but it was hard when Ellen just pulled people in. Even in her mid-fifties, she was svelte and stunning, her hair never seeming to be out of place and not a grey hair in sight. She looked far younger than she actually was, although Miles thought she would be stunning no matter what she looked like.

The damn woman was a tease as well. It was like she knew how Miles felt about her and dangled a carrot in front of him. She would draw him in and then toss him away once she had had her fun. It wasn't just Miles she did that with, either. How Jake put up with a flirt for a wife when he was a straight-laced person, Miles had no idea.

Jake didn't deserve Ellen. Neither did Miles, if it came to it. But he couldn't stop himself with the way he felt.

He checked his phone again, smiling as he saw the texts from Ellen.

I've just pulled up. Are you here? Can't see your car. X

It was a moment later that he got a response.

I parked up at the master's house. And I'm already inside. Door's unlocked. X

Miles really liked it when she put kisses on her texts. It was silly, and it was a small thing, but it made him feel good.

God, he was such a sap.

Getting out, Miles locked up the car and went into the workshop. He passed the rooms that housed the computers and into the main workshop. His hand went automatically to the light switches, but there were a few clicks when he flicked them and nothing happened. Miles tried again, and still nothing.

Damn. Of all the times for the lights to not work...

No matter. He could make his way around the workshop with his eyes closed. And there was enough moonlight coming through the windows. This shouldn't be a problem. Just as long as the security guard didn't wander by the workshop at the wrong moment. Ellen is very vocal, and Miles didn't want them to be interrupted.

Miles adjusted his crotch as his cock hardened, pressing against his zipper. It was really hard to work around Ellen, especially when she kept walking around in figure-hugging clothes. She kept herself in very good shape. And that backside of hers was enough to keep Miles' wet dreams going for days.

Now I'm going to be inside her. It feels so long since...

The sound of a drill being turned on jerked Miles out of his thoughts. He spun around towards the workbench, and for a moment he didn't see anyone. Then there was a movement by the bench, deep in the shadows that the moonlight couldn't reach. Miles squinted, trying to see what was there. For a moment, it was just blackness, nothing else.

Then the shadows shifted, and the outline of someone got up from the stool. Miles couldn't see their face, but he saw that they had long hair.

Ellen. Miles smiled and stepped towards her.

"It's been a while since we've been alone, hasn't it? Sorry about the lights, but..." he faltered as the other person moved closer, and his eyes adjusted to the dark. "Wait, what are you...?"

There was a blur, and something was shoved against his chest. Instantaneously, Miles felt a strong surge of electricity through his body that made everything tingle. Then his legs gave way beneath him, and he found himself falling, unable to put his arms out to save himself.

A flash of pain in his head sucked him into the shadows around him, and then Miles didn't feel anything else.

* * *

The pain was the first thing Miles was aware of. It felt like his head had been split open, and his skull was pulsating. He felt really lightheaded.

Then he realised that he was lying on his back, his arms spread wide. He could move his fingers, but he couldn't move his arms. Same with his toes; they were able to wriggle, and yet Miles couldn't lift his legs.

He could lift his head, though. Gingerly raising it, even with everything screaming at him not to move, Miles looked over himself. He was lying on the worktable in the middle of the workshop. He didn't seem to be tied down with anything, but he couldn't move any part of his body. He couldn't even lift his hands off the table, his skin screaming at him as he tried.

Shit. Someone had glued him down to the table.

Miles began to panic. He tried to scream, only to find that he couldn't open his mouth. His lips wouldn't move, and red-hot pain shot through the lower part of his face when he tried to pry his mouth open. Had whoever did this glued his mouth together as well?

The lights above him turned on suddenly, and Miles blinked and tried to turn his head away. Damn, that hurt. It felt like little pinpricks were searing into his eyes. He tried to scream again, but it just sounded muffled. Even if the groundskeeper was doing his rounds, he wouldn't be able to hear anything; the workshop was insulated to make it soundproof.

Nobody would be coming to help him.

Stay calm. It's just a prank. You'll get released in the morning, and you'll be fine.

Even as he told himself that, Miles knew that this wasn't a prank. Pranks didn't include pinning him to a table with industrial-strength glue.

Fuck. Where was the bitch who knocked him out? She had done something to make him pass out. Had she stuck a taser into his chest? He could have been killed.

Where the fuck was she?

Footsteps reached his ears, soft on the wooden floor but loud enough in the silent room that Miles immediately searched for the noise. Someone was approaching him, dressed in black from the balaclava to the gloved hands and the sneakers. All of it generic, no indicating marks. And from the way the clothes fitted, Miles had no idea if it was the woman who had knocked him out, no sign of long hair. It could have been a wig, for all he knew.

Had someone pretended to be Ellen to lure him in? But how did they get Ellen's number? Was she in on this as well?

Miles went cold. Shit, had something happened to Ellen? Was she in danger?

He tried to speak again, his words coming out in muffled snarls. But there was no reaction from the figure. They just watched him, eyes looking like there were holes in the mask.

This was definitely not a prank. Miles could feel goosebumps coming up all over his body.

Shit. Was he going to die?

Don't panic. You can get out of this. Just don't freak out.

The stranger moved, walking like they were gliding on water. Miles tried to follow them, hoping to see something that told him who it was. Anything at all. Then they moved out of sight, and Miles tried to lean his head back to look behind him, only to bang his head against the table. The pain in his head threatened to drag him into unconsciousness again, and Miles felt the nausea in his stomach. The smell of the glue and the pain in his head were not a good combination.

He could only hope he didn't throw up and choked on his own vomit.

The sound of a blade being switched on brought Miles back to his senses. Breathing heavily through his nose, he looked around trying to see the black-masked stranger, but that just made the glue sticking to his t-shirt twist, and it felt like his skin was burning. A moment later, the stranger moved into view, and Miles saw what he was holding.

An angle grinder, and the blade was spinning so fast that Miles couldn't see the serrated edge.

Oh, fuck. They aren't...

Miles wasn't expecting the sudden slice on his thigh. His jeans barely softened the impact, and pain shot through his leg. Miles screamed, the glue on his mouth not budging, and it just added to the pain. Holy hell, the last time he had been sliced like that had been when he was at school himself and he cut his arm open. Even then, that wasn't as painful as what he was feeling right now.

The stranger swiped at him again, this time on Miles' stomach. Miles hissed. Shit, that was even worse. The burn was more intense. He looked down and saw the red line across his soft belly.

And that was just superficial. What was going to happen if it went any...?

Miles' whole body jolted as the grinder was pressed against his chest. And it went in. Miles screamed and watched in horror as the grinder actually sank into his chest. Blood splattered his face, cold against his cheeks and jaw. He wanted to wipe it away, but he couldn't.

Panic was not being held back anymore. It was building, and Miles was sure he was going to be sick. Knowing that he couldn't actually throw up made him panic even more.

He might as well have glued up his nose as he struggled to breathe when the grinder came out. Then it was turned off and put on the counter. It was then that Miles noticed that there was a long white container. He could see the word 'salt' curling around the side of the bottle.

Had that been there before? And why was the guy – if it was a guy – picking it up?

Miles felt like his breath had gotten stuck in his throat as he watched his torturer unscrew the lid of the salt and put it on the table. Then they leaned over very slowly, turning a steely gaze on Miles. The look in his eyes was terrifying.

It was pure fury.

Slowly, almost like they had all the time in the world, they lifted the salt bottle and sprinkled a long, straight line next to the wound on Miles' chest. Not touching, but very close. A stray few pieces landed on the wound, and Miles gritted his teeth as he felt it sting. Blood was now pooling on his chest, mixing with the salt crystals. He could feel it trickling down by his neck, and it was itching.

Their eyes met again, and Miles was sure his heart had stopped. Neither of them moved, both turned into statues. Miles really wanted to scream, to fight the bastard off and get out of there.

This has to be a really bad dream. I'm going to wake up in a minute.

The salt getting pushed into the cut on his chest was even more excruciating than the angle grinder slicing him open. Miles' chest felt like it burned. He could feel the gloved fingers pressing along the cut, the burn getting worse.

Suddenly, the fingers pulled away, leaving Miles' whole body feeling like it was on fire. He was close to hyperventilating, bile rising up in his throat. He needed to breathe. He had to.

But he couldn't. He couldn't get the fuck away.

Barely able to lift his head, Miles watched as the salt was picked up and tilted over his stomach. Miles tried to plead, attempting to force his mouth apart. The glue was beginning to lose its strength. Would he be able to get his mouth free?

Ungluing his mouth momentarily left his thoughts as the salt was sprinkled right over his wound, a hand slapping on top and rubbing hard. Shit, this was too much.

Then the stranger put the salt back on the counter, which had Miles heaving a sigh of relief. He had a reprieve. It wouldn't be much, but enough that he could gather his thoughts. There had to be a way out of this somehow.

However, deep down, Miles knew he wasn't getting out of this.

This wasn't meant to happen tonight. How had he ended up going from a romantic rendezvous to becoming the victim of a sadist's torture?

There was a rustling of paper, and Miles looked over. The stranger was carefully placing a photograph against the pencil holder, angling it so Miles could see it clearly. It took a moment for him to recognize the girl in the picture. It had been pinned up on the wall in the staffroom. That little girl from all those years ago.

What is going on with that?

It was then that Miles had a memory of what happened in the workshop. So long ago that it slowly materialised to him. A memory where the girl had to go to matron because she was cut badly by an angle grinder, something he was told was an accident. Miles recalled putting her in another part of the workshop because she wasn't safe with any of the equipment. She hadn't meant to be using it, and she still injured herself.

Even then, she couldn't keep out of trouble. Her hair got so much glue in it that she had to have it shaved almost down to the scalp. Her classmates had said nothing bad happened, and Miles had let it go.

Because you knew what was happening to her. You knew she was a target, and you let it happen anyway.

All because they told you this was the right thing to do. And you followed them like a pathetic sheep.

Miles was jerked out of remembering that poor kid who did nothing wrong except be an accessible target by the sound of a bottle cap coming undone. His torturer had picked up a big bottle of something, taking off the cap.

Miles recognised the bottle. It was the bleach that the cleaners used to mop the floor.

Shit, was this bastard actually going to...

He struggled, thinking that he might be able to get free if he kept trying. But it was useless. There was no getting out of this.

The open bottle of bleach was placed beside him, and the angle grinder was picked up and switched on. The sound of the whirling blade made Miles flinch. Then it was lowered to his wrist.

Miles wanted to pull his hand away, but he couldn't, and the only thing he could do was watch as the blade went in deep into his wrist.

Chapter Seven

Monday 27th November 2000

I cried when I saw J when she came back today. Her long hair had been cut short. They tried to style it to make it look cute, but it doesn't look right on her. How she didn't get injured from that, I have no idea.

They said she had been playing around with the glue. Who plays with hot glue by pouring it over their head? Then they said it was an accident. Like when they picked up the angle grinder and chased her around the workshop until they sliced her arm.

J always hated DT. She told me she was too scared to go into the workshop now. She wanted to find a way not to go in, but she would be forced. And PB would torment her. Again.

It's always that fucking bitch.

If only I had been there. I could have told them it wasn't, and Mr S looked the other way. But nobody would listen to me. Mum and Dad would, but they wouldn't be able to do anything. QB is in charge, and nobody gets to argue against her.

Mr S is weak and pathetic. He knew, and he said nothing. Mum told me of a phrase that seems to be quite fitting: rubbing salt into the wound. It means making a difficult situation even worse for someone. He's making this worse for J. He isn't stupid. He does know what happened to her.

And he chose to say nothing. What a prick.

* * *

Ellen really didn't want to do this. She could have done with a few extra minutes in bed, cuddled up to Jake as he snored away. If he woke first, he would roll over and they could snuggle for a bit before one of them had to get up. Even when they argued, that never stopped.

And Ellen had missed it that morning. All because she had agreed to see Miles before anyone got to school that morning. He would have been very insistent until she did as he wanted. Ellen did not bow down to anyone, not even her husband. Miles did not get to order her around.

She would be having a few choice words to say to him for doing this.

Thankfully, nobody was around, although she saw David's car parked in the headteacher's space by the front door. Shit, why did he have to come in early? He was taking his role as acting head very seriously if he was here long before anyone needed to be.

Not for the first time, Ellen hoped that they would get the hierarchy sorted again with the teachers. Some of the younger ones were forgetting their place, and the experienced teachers were getting sidelined. Ellen liked David but he was still relatively new to Wolsey Prep. He thought being a teacher wasn't that hard, but he hadn't been the headteacher then.

Ellen wondered how long it would be before David gave up and left.

Pulling up as quietly as she could at the far end of the car park, she got out and slung her handbag over her shoulder. It was a particularly warm day again, even at seven in the morning, and Ellen had seen that the forecast said it would be hotter later. Even so, Ellen could feel sweat trickling down her back, her dress sticking to her legs after sitting in the car.

Her underwear was going to need to be peeled off her, if it got any hotter.

Trying to ignore the feel of her clothes moulding to her body in a way that it wasn't supposed to, Ellen hurried over to the DT building and tried the door. It was open. Glancing around her and satisfied that nobody was in sight, Ellen went in, closing the door quietly behind her.

The building was still. There didn't seem to be any sound at all, not even the whirring of the computers running on rest mode. Her footsteps echoed in her ears as Ellen crossed the cloakroom towards the double doors into the main workshop. If Miles was here, he would be there, in his office at the back. He was always working on something, almost like a kid in a sweet shop. His enthusiasm was almost adorable.

Almost.

But Ellen didn't get that far before she saw the body on the centre table, lying on their back staring at the ceiling. She could see the blood under the body.

It took her a moment to realise who it was in front of her.

Unable to comprehend what she was seeing, Ellen knew she should turn around and run. Find a phone and call for help. Find David and tell him what had happened. She shouldn't go anywhere near this.

But she found herself shoving open the door to the workshop and running inside, stopping at the table and looking down at the wide, horrified eyes of Miles.

She didn't need to look at his face to know that he was dead. The deep gouge in his throat, looking like a second mouth, was a pretty clear indication of what had killed him. But the rest of his body...his t-shirt was ripped to shreds, and there were rips in his jeans. Bloody pooled on the denim, some of the wounds looking deep. They were the same on his chest as well, including the deep cuts on his wrists and arms. Someone had really gone to town on him. There was also something scattered on the table, mixed in with the blood. They looked like crystals.

Salt crystals. What the hell had happened here?

Panic squeezing her chest and closing her throat, Ellen put her hands to her mouth and tried to fight back the scream that was building. Someone had butchered Miles, slicing him up like a hunk of meat.

He had been tortured.

Oh, God. Not Miles.

Get out of here. Now.

Stumbling back, Ellen bumped into the table behind her, which knocked her onto the floor. Her hands landed in something sticky and cold. To her horror, she saw that she had put her hands into the blood splattered across the floor.

Ellen felt like she was going to be sick. Scrambling to her feet, the strap of her handbag now dangling off her arm, she tried to leave the room without openly staring at Miles. He looked so creepy like that, his throat sliced open with his mouth somehow contorted with his lips together, his eyes wide and unblinking. Even then, it felt like his eyes were following her.

Bile started to burn her throat, and Ellen fell to her knees again as she gave in to the urge to throw up. Her stomach heaved, and it didn't want to stop. Ellen started feeling dizzy, and everything tilted sharply to the side. She collapsed onto the floor, her eyes shut as she desperately waited for the world to stop spinning. But it didn't get the image of Miles out of her head.

Get out of there!

"Jesus Christ!"

It took a moment for Ellen to realise that someone else was there. She gingerly blinked her eyes open, only to groan and cover her eyes with her hands as the world shifted again and threatened to make her vomit again.

Was that David? Had he seen her coming in here? Everything was pounding in her head. It felt like there was a ringing in her ears. Ellen rolled onto her side and curled into a ball. Fuck, this felt like a horrible nightmare. Was she going to wake up anytime soon?

Footsteps reached her ears, and Ellen braced herself, lowering her hands to see David moving towards Miles' body. His body was tense as he stared in silence at the mess. Ellen had no idea how he could look at the state without reacting badly. Then he flexed his hands and turned, his expression grim. His eyes widened when he saw her staring at her.

"Ellen!" He rushed over to her and knelt beside her. "What happened?"

"I...I don't know." Ellen allowed him to help her sit up. "I...I just...oh, God..."

She couldn't look at Miles, but her attention was snagged by the mess. Instead, she looked at her hands, only to see the blood covering them.

"Your face..." David reached out and touched her chin, turning her to look at him. "You weren't hurt, were you?"

"No. No, I wasn't." Ellen shook her head, but that just made the pounding worse. "It's not mine."

Something flashed in David's eyes. Then he took her arm.

"Do you want some help getting up?"

"I...I think I do..." Ellen pressed a hand to her chest, trying to breathe properly. But it wasn't working. "Everything is...I feel like I'm going to be sick again."

"Then let's get you somewhere else. And I need to call the police." David grasped her under the shoulders and lifted Ellen to her feet. "I'll call an ambulance for you as well..."

"No!" Ellen shook her head, only to groan when her head hurt even more. "I don't need an ambulance."

"Ellen, you've just had a shock..."

"And I said no! Just get me away from this!"

Ellen didn't want to do anything except get out of there. And with the way her legs were feeling, she was probably not going to leave on her own. Not comfortably, anyway.

David looked like he wanted to argue with her, but he nodded and tucked her into his side.

"Just lean on me," he said quietly, putting her arm around his shoulders. "I'll take you somewhere else."

Ellen did as she was told, doing her best not to look back at the body that had been Miles Sims.

Chapter Eight

Elizabeth's heart leapt when she saw David's car parked outside the school. Then she silently cursed herself. Damn, she was going to end up with an obsession that was going to get her into serious trouble. If only it would stop.

At least she would be able to meet David and talk to him like any other person instead of someone she had stuck up on a pedestal.

Ellen had told her before that crushes were healthy but there was a line, and you had to be aware of where the line was before it became blurred. It sounded like she had been speaking from personal experience. Elizabeth thought that it would never happen to her. She was a confident woman; she knew what she wanted.

So why did she fumble over a man like David Barlow? What was wrong with her?

Just get inside and get to work. Don't interact with him unless you have to. He'll probably be too busy to talk, anyway.

It was annoying that they had to come into work in the middle of the holidays. Elizabeth wanted to spend more time going on holiday with her friends. She was missing a trip to Sweden for this. But the boarders would be arriving in a week, and everything needed to be sorted. If the lesson plans were done now, then all that was needed to worry about was the teacher training day the Friday before the terms started. Isabella said it was best to get it done before the students started arriving, otherwise they would be doing more time babysitting than getting prepared.

Much as Elizabeth loved her job, she wished that she didn't have to deal with kids. Stupid brats, and those ones from the upper prep were probably the worst going through puberty. They were so irritating.

She had been a bitch, but she hadn't been that bad.

Putting her bag on her chair behind the reception desk, Elizabeth checked her phone as she switched on the laptop. Nothing coming in so far. Not even a text message from her family. Hadn't her mum said she would call to ask when she was going to come down to London soon? She was not normally forgetful.

She would call later, providing the signal actually decided to work. It wasn't really important right now.

Putting her phone down and leaving the laptop to boot up, Elizabeth went into the staffroom to check her pigeon hole. Halfway there, she stopped when she remembered that there was not going to be any post. With the school being closed, if any post came it would be going to the groundskeeper in the old master's house up at the other end of the school.

Which meant she would have to make her way up there to get the damn stuff.

Sighing heavily, Elizabeth started to turn away, only to spot something in her pigeon hole. She turned back. Had that envelope been there before? She couldn't recall having missed something. Taking the tan-coloured paper out, she turned it over. It had her name neatly printed on the front, along with the school's address.

Maybe she did forget it.

She ripped open the seal and dug inside, only to feel a sudden sting of pain on her wrist. Flinching, Elizabeth pulled her hand away and stared at the line of red coming up along her skin.

Fuck. Papercuts hurt so much. Of all the places to get one...

Sucking on her wrist, Elizabeth used one hand to peek into the envelope. There just seemed to be a piece of paper. Much smaller than its packaging. Going over to the table, she tipped the contents onto the stained oak.

Oh, God. Not another one. A picture of that girl again, only it wasn't a school photograph. This time, she was standing by a swimming pool in t-shirt and shorts, her hair wet and beaming with three medals around her neck. She looked happier than Elizabeth had ever seen her.

Just looking at the picture made Elizabeth feel sick. It brought back memories of that day, when things took a turn and tarnished the whole day.

It was a time Elizabeth didn't want to think about. And she certainly didn't want a picture of that little bitch. The day was ruined enough, as it is.

She ripped up the photograph, along with the envelope. Then she dropped both into the bin. It would get buried under everything else, and then she wouldn't have to worry about seeing that face again.

Her wrist was beginning to sting. Elizabeth inspected it. It was just a scratch, but it was quite long. A tiny bit of blood was building along the cut.

Great. Just what she needed right now. And where was the first-aid box when she needed it?

Elizabeth went back to the front desk. There had to be a first-aid box in one of the drawers. She had seen it only yesterday. It was just a matter of trying to find it.

If only she was more organised as an adult.

But there was something pinned to the computer that caught Elizabeth's attention first. Another damn picture, only this time it was of the same girl playing the violin. From the backdrop, it had to have been taken on the terrace at one of the recitals. She was focused on the music, her violin looking far too big for her.

What the hell was going on here?

Growling, Elizabeth tried to yank the picture off the desktop, but it only resulted in almost taking the computer with her as the sellotape refused to yield. She caught it before the desktop came off its stand and put it back where it was supposed to be. This time, she carefully peeled the photograph off and stared at the girl.

Whoever thought it was funny to leave these pictures lying around were going to get into serious trouble. Elizabeth had no sense of humour for something like this.

And she certainly didn't want to be reminded of this girl.

Voices outside jerked Elizabeth out of her daze. Aware that people were coming, she opened the top drawer and shoved the picture inside before snapping it shut. That could be dealt with later. She looked up just as David and Ellen came staggering in. Elizabeth was about to give both a greeting, only for it to die when she saw the state of Ellen.

Holy fuck, what happened to her? She had blood on the front of her dress, on her legs, her hands, even her face. But Elizabeth couldn't see any signs of injury. Yet the look of shock on her face, her pale complexion...

She hurried around the desk.

"What's happened?"

"Call the police, Elizabeth," David said through gritted teeth, hoisting Ellen up as she started to buckle a little. "Tell them there's been another murder."

"*What?*"

"Just call! I'll direct them when they get here." David spoke over his shoulder as he led Ellen towards his office. "Be quick about it! Then when you're done, find Hector and tell him to lock the DT workshop up. I don't want anyone going in there."

The DT workshop? What the hell was going on? But Elizabeth could tell that she wouldn't get her answers yet. Snatching up the phone, she began to dial. It felt like forever before there was an answer from the operator. Elizabeth had no idea what to say. She was still remembering how bloodied and messy Ellen looked when she came in. Had she been attacked?

But wait...David said to report a murder. Did that mean...?

"Elizabeth?"

Elizabeth jumped. Leanne was standing on the other side of the desk, looking at her oddly. Elizabeth hadn't noticed her come in, and you could normally hear Leanne coming from a mile away. The bitch liked to make her presence known.

Leanne was frowning at her, gesturing at the phone.

"Are you okay? You haven't moved since I came in."

"What?"

Then Elizabeth realised what she was doing. The operator had hung up on her end; she must have thought it was a prank call. Putting the receiver back, Elizabeth tried again. Leanne peered at her.

"What's going on? You look a little spooked."

"I'm not sure, if I'm honest." Elizabeth hated not having any answers. "Could you go and find Hector? The DT workshop needs to be locked."

"What? Why?"

"I don't know. I'm just doing what David asked of me. Can you do that?"

"I...sure. Of course." Leanne put her bag on the desk and headed towards the door, her flowy skirt wafting about her legs. "This better not be what I think it is."

Elizabeth didn't respond. From Ellen's appearance, it was very much what they thought it was.

And now they had to find out who had been murdered. Elizabeth found that she didn't really want to know.

* * *

Miles was dead. Ellen had that going through her head, repeated again and again until the words blurred together. She had seen his body, seen how he clearly couldn't be alive. And yet it didn't seem real.

The blood on her face and hands were beginning to tickle. It was like she had face paint on and it began to irritate the skin after a while. The police had taken samples from her already, along with her dress for testing. At least Leanne had a spare change of clothes with her in the car, which Ellen was grateful about. For the first time, she was glad that Leanne was a little too organised and carried a bag of clothes around with her. In her words, 'you never know when you might need something'.

Ellen doubted that Leanne thought her clothes would be used to replace those that had been bloodied at a crime scene, though.

Her stomach churned at the memory of seeing Miles cut up like that. Someone had really gone to town on him. He had looked horrified, and the expression on his face...

Poor Miles. He didn't deserve that.

"Mrs Lawson?"

Ellen looked up. A tall, thin man with a bald head and trim dark beard was standing by the desk. Wait, when had he entered the room? He approached her, giving her a gentle smile.

"Mrs Lawson, I'm Detective Inspector Franks. I know you've given a statement, but I do have some more questions for you."

"Oh. Right."

"Are you sure this can't wait until later?" David's voice made Ellen jump. She had even forgotten that he was in the room. He was leaning against the desk with his arms folded, not looking too impressed. "Mrs Lawson is in shock. She should be at home."

"I'm afraid it can't. The sooner we do this, the sooner we can get the more vital information." Inspector Franks caused. "Also, there is something that we need to ask, and as Mrs Lawson has been at this school a long time, I thought she would be the best person to talk to."

Ellen wasn't sure she liked where this was going. And after giving her statement - that felt like a lifetime ago - she didn't want to talk about Miles. She could still remember his face, as if he could actually see her standing there. Almost accusatory.

She wasn't sure if his face was worse than Isabella's or not. Her stomach was empty, and it was threatening to bring up whatever there was left.

"Ellen." David frowned at her. "Seriously, you don't have to do this now. I'll make sure you're left alone..."

"It's okay, David." It wasn't, but Ellen just wanted everyone to go away. She managed a tiny smile. "As long as it's quick, it should be fine."

David still didn't look convinced. Inspector Franks eased his frame into the armchair next to Ellen. He looked like one of those people who could snap in half if the wind blew the wrong way at the wrong moment. Ellen wondered if that was even possible. It wouldn't be the first time she had seen bodies go into positions that shouldn't happen naturally.

Then she noticed that the inspector was carrying something in his hand. A slim piece of paper was inside an evidence bag, but Ellen couldn't see what was on it. Mostly because his long, slim fingers were in the way.

Ellen really wanted to ask how Miles had died, but then she recalled the slashed throat. And she didn't want the details of what happened before he died. Nevertheless, her curiosity was beginning to get the better of her.

"Mrs Lawson..."

"Why did Miles' face look so odd, Inspector?"

Inspector Franks blinked.

"I'm sorry?"

"His mouth looked...strange. I don't know how to describe it. If he was laid out on the bench, why didn't he fight his attacker off? And why didn't he scream for help?"

"I think it's best that you don't know," David said quietly.

Ellen glared at him.

"I'm not a child, David. And I want to know. The least the inspector can do is answer my question."

The inspector didn't look too keen on it, though. Finally, he sighed.

"He didn't fight anyone off because he was glued down to the table."

"What?"

"His entire body was stuck to the table with very strong

81

glue. We've only just got him separated from the wood." He hesitated. "And his mouth was glued together. It had partly come undone on one side, but even that pulling apart would have been...well..."

Would have been excruciating. That's what he would have said. Ellen wanted to cry again, but she didn't think she had any strength left. She didn't think she had felt so weak as she had in the last couple of days.

There is one time you did feel weak. When you made that mistake...

I will not think about that.

"We found this propped up against the workbench near where Mr Sims was killed. We don't really know what it means, but we think it could be a connection." He turned the evidence bag around. "Do you recognise the girl in this photograph, Mrs Lawson?"

Ellen's heart stopped when she saw it again. That school picture of the smiling child. Not this again. That had been near Miles' body? But hadn't she put it in the shredder?

"Mrs Lawson?"

Inspector Franks was looking at her expectantly. Ellen swallowed.

"You think I know this girl?"

"Well, she's wearing the school uniform. I asked Mr Barlow, but he said he didn't know who it was. I could go into the archives if you don't recall her..."

"I know who she is."

The words were out before Ellen could stop them. David's eyes narrowed, and Inspector Franks shifted forwards a little.

"Who is she? Is she a current student?"

"No. She's been dead for over twenty years."

82

Just saying those words left a nasty taste in Ellen's mouth. All of the memories of that time came back, and they weren't pleasant. Now the inspector looked interested.

"What can you tell me about her?"

What could she tell him? Ellen wished she had said she didn't know, but that lie would have been found out. She was going to be found out this time.

You did nothing wrong. Take a deep breath and tell them the basics.

"Her name is Jane Christian. She came here for the school year in 2000. Her father was the bursar at the college, and her mother was a music teacher. She also helped out with the hockey teams."

"What school year was she in?" Inspector Franks asked.

"Just year seven. She was only here for nine months."

"What happened?"

Ellen stared at the picture, at the smiling girl looking back at her. So innocent, and yet...

"She died. Got hit with a car. The police never found the driver."

"I see." Inspector Franks tilted his head to one side as if regarding her differently. Ellen wished that he wouldn't. "What happened to the family?"

"They left. Took her brother and went back to...I think it was Derbyshire? I didn't interact with the mother. She was a little too aloof. Thought she was better than everyone else."

"Was that how Jane was as well?"

Ellen nodded.

"She was rather uppity. A bright girl, but uppity. I didn't think much of her. She was a bit of a loner because of her attitude, though. Barely had any friends."

"And the day she died? Do you know what happened?"

Ellen was aware of David staring at her, but the look he gave her was blank. Even so, it was disquieting. She shook her head.

"I don't really know. It was the day of an athletics tournament we had on the grounds. Everyone was here, parents and students. Then we heard a commotion and found Jane by the changing rooms. The inquest said she had been hit by a car and thrown into a wall, and that broke a rib which perforated her lung. She died drowning in her own blood."

Even now recalling that left her feeling nauseous. Ellen couldn't imagine a worse way to die. Then she remembered Isabella and Miles, and wondered if that was the lesser of some evils.

"Are you thinking that the parents might be involved in this, Inspector?" David asked. "That they killed Mrs Sanders and Mr Sims?"

"It's a stretch, but there is a definite link between the two murders. Two in two days? That's not a coincidence."

"And this Jane Christian is the link?"

Inspector Franks looked unsure.

"At this moment in time, we can only speculate. And I don't really want to do that." He turned back to Ellen. "Mrs Lawson, is there anything else you can tell us about this girl? Were the victims here twenty-three years ago when she was?"

Ellen nodded.

"Mr Sims is - was - our IT and DT teacher. He's been here for thirty years. Mrs Sanders started in 1999."

"So they would have interacted with Jane Christian."

"She was in upper prep, so yes." Ellen frowned. "You really do think these are linked by that girl, don't you?"

"I'm just covering all the bases, Mrs Lawson. The fact that

the girl's picture was found at both scenes…"

"Wait, what?" Ellen shook her head. "There wasn't a picture of Jane yesterday when I found Isabella. I would have said something."

"I found it."

Ellen looked at David. He reached behind him and tapped the desk.

"It was lying on the desk. I gave it to the police yesterday."

Ellen hadn't known that. How did she not see it?

"You never told me," she murmured.

"Everything happened so fast, and you were both in shock," Inspector Franks reminded her.

He had a point, but Ellen was still staring at David, who was watching the inspector with a clenched jaw. He was holding himself together well, given the circumstances, but he was clearly angry. Having this happen when he was meant to be in charge had to be embarrassing for him.

"Thank you for your help, Mrs Lawson." The inspector pushed himself up with a groan. "I'll be in touch. I think it's best that everyone goes home. This place is going to be a crime scene for a while."

David's frown darkened.

"We have work we need to do, Inspector. The students are coming in next week. If we're not ready…"

"This school is a crime scene now, Mr Barlow."

"Again?"

Inspector Franks held up his hands.

"I'm sorry, but it can't be helped. I would advise everyone coming in to go home and do what they can from there. Hopefully, we'll finish in time for the students to arrive without any issues. But we can't do that until all of you cooperate with me."

Ellen could tell that David was upset about that. He didn't like things being out of his control. She stood up, smoothing down the baggy black trousers Leanne had given her.

"We'll do what you wish, Inspector," she said. "Anything to help you find who killed Isabella and Miles."

If they were lucky, they would be able to find out who was killing everyone, and why it felt like everyone who knew Jane Christian was going to have a target on their back going forward.

Chapter Nine

They had to go home. Again. Elizabeth was beginning to think they were never going to get any of this over with. She would rather go home and stay home rather than keep going back and forth from her house. It was a good thing she didn't need to go far, otherwise it would be a real waste of time. But she could understand why the police didn't want anyone around; the place was turning into an abattoir.

It was hard to believe that Miles Sims had been murdered. And in such a horrific fashion. Elizabeth had eavesdropped on Ellen while she was giving her statement, and to hear how Miles had been found was shocking. God, she couldn't begin to imagine who had the stomach to do something disgusting. And to Miles as well; he had been one of her favourite teachers. Elizabeth was fond of him.

Now he was gone. Never coming back.

Who would kill him? Elizabeth didn't understand. Miles didn't have any enemies; he was too nice for that. What she had overheard suggested that it was personal.

Either that or there was someone sadistic running around in the Suffolk countryside. Elizabeth liked watching horror movies, but she didn't want to be in one. That was too much.

David was still talking to the police with Ellen when Elizabeth was told that she could go home. Elizabeth wanted to stay and see if he needed anything, but she was advised that it would be best for everyone to leave as soon as possible. Her statement had been taken, so she didn't need to stay for anything, and David was more than likely going to take a while.

Elizabeth just wanted to see if he was okay.

No, that's your crush telling you to stay. Just be a grown-up and leave.

Heading out to her car, Elizabeth got in and sat for a moment, watching the police milling around outside the DT building. There were sounds of machinery coming from there, even with the doors closed. What on earth were they doing in there? Elizabeth wasn't sure she wanted to know.

Turning the engine on, she drove down the drive towards the exit, but as she approached, Elizabeth's attention went to the turning off to the left. This route went along adjacent to the wall to another car park, and towards the playing fields and the changing rooms. More open space with a third exit from the school grounds.

It would be quiet right now. No one to bother her.

Making a decision, Elizabeth turned to the left, and drove towards the playing fields. Nobody seemed to notice her go, and she didn't see anyone around. Elizabeth parked on the grass and put the car into neutral with the handbrake on. Then she sat there, staring at the view before her.

Her gaze kept going to the house just by the changing rooms, surrounded by a hedge. It was a little odd having a house separate from the school in the grounds, but it had been there for years. The old master's house, which was now used for the head groundskeeper and his family so they had someone on hand to look after the place. It hadn't always been like that. Her former maths teacher and his family had used the house for a few years. Such a long time ago now. Elizabeth remembered feeling a little jealous at how gorgeous the house was. Nothing like that in London.

The playing fields stretched out beyond the house, a wide expanse of green at this time of year. There had been many memories of this part of the school. Scoring goals in hockey, winning cross-country races and being the best batter in rounders. The tennis courts where she would practise for hours to win with ease. All good memories, ones that made Elizabeth smile. She had thrived for sports; they made her feel good.

But there was also a memory that refused to leave. One that overshadowed everything if she allowed it. And Elizabeth's eyes kept going back to the changing rooms, the simple red brick building that looked a lot bigger than it was on the inside.

This was where Jane Christian had died. Where she had been hit by a car and thrown against the wall. Elizabeth remembered seeing her body and how her body had been at an odd angle, her eyes open and sightless, seeming to look right through her.

No, she would not think about that. It left Elizabeth feeling like her skin was crawling. Not her finest memory.

Would she still be alive if she hadn't been killed? Would she have gone on to do something with her life? She certainly hadn't done much with it in the twelve years before her death. Elizabeth didn't think she would have made much of a significant impact on anything.

She certainly made a significant impact after her death. Even from the grave she taunted.

If they had known everything, though...

A rap on the window made her memories explode into a thousand pieces, and Elizabeth almost screamed. It took her a moment to focus on the man leaning over, peering in through her window. A familiar man with red hair tied back in a ponytail, wearing those thick black-rimmed glasses that looked like they had seen better days. He was frowning at her, gesturing at her to roll the window down.

Her heart still racing, Elizabeth fumbled for the button and the window went down. Dominic Holloway started speaking as soon as there was a gap for warm air to come in.

"Are you okay, Elizabeth?"

Elizabeth scowled.

"I was doing okay until you scared the shit out of me."

"Sorry. You were staring into space. I thought you'd gone already, so when I saw you here..."

"You thought it would be a good time to bother me?"

The science teacher blushed almost as red as his hair. Elizabeth eased back on her frustration. Dominic was one of the newer teachers, and while he was brilliant and the kids loved him, he was probably the most sensitive person she had met in a long time. He liked to overthink situations, and he got upset if someone was mad. He didn't have a thick skin at all once the kids were out of the classroom.

Much like Jane. She didn't have a thick skin. It's why she was an easy target.

"I'm sorry, Dominic." Elizabeth fumbled for the door handle and got out, Dominic easing back to give her some room. "It's just with two murders in two days, and everything disrupting our lives, I'm in a bit of a mess."

"I guess everyone's really on edge right now." Dominic rubbed the back of his neck. "I can't blame them. After all, there's a sadist running around and we don't know who it is."

"You think he's sadistic?"

"He has to be. One of my friends is on the forensic team, and we were talking. He said that Miles had had salt rubbed into his wounds, quite literally, and there were burns from bleach all over his body."

Elizabeth's stomach clenched. She hadn't heard that part, and the idea of having salt and bleach tipped over her made her shudder.

"Someone really wanted him to suffer," she commented.

"But who? Miles was a decent guy. A bit of a pushover, but decent."

"A pushover?"

Dominic shrugged.

"I've been here a little over a year now, and I've noticed how Miles doesn't have any drive or ability to stand up for himself when he's not teaching the kids. Especially when it comes to Ellen Lawson."

Elizabeth folded her arms.

"Are you implying that Miles and Ellen...? She's married! Jake's a decent guy!"

"I'm not saying they've had an affair or anything, but Miles clearly had a crush on her." Dominic raised his hands. "From the way she treats him, Ellen knows and dangles a carrot in front of him."

"That's no way to talk about a respected member of the staff, Dominic. Ellen is our standout teacher here."

Dominic's expression said he didn't believe that, but he wisely didn't say anything more. Elizabeth wouldn't have taken it; Ellen had seen her potential and pushed her to do her best. She wouldn't have a word said against the woman who made her as she was.

A lot of blood, sweat and tears had been put into Elizabeth's schooling, and it had paid off. Ellen was the reason for it.

"What are you doing out here, anyway?" Elizabeth asked. "I saw you come in, and then you disappeared."

"I spoke to an officer, but I didn't have much to add, so I went for a walk." Dominic gave her a sheepish smile, almost embarrassed. "I'm a bit of a wimp when it comes to dead things. Hearing that someone I know is dead..."

"I get it." Elizabeth understood, more than he could know. "You're going to have to vacate the school grounds soon. Everyone's been told to go home. David said there's no point trying to keep coming in to get our pre-school work done, so we should stay at home and get as much as we can done there."

"I just need to do an inventory of the chemicals in the back room, and then I'll go home."

"Can't that wait until term starts?"

Dominic shook his head.

"No, I'm afraid not. When I was talking to the officer, we were in my classroom. I was doing a cursory check of the storage room, and I saw that there was less hydrochloric acid than expected. I always have everything topped up before I leave for the holidays, and I had one bottle left."

Elizabeth frowned.

"You're more concerned about inventory?"

"Hydrochloric acid is very corrosive, Elizabeth, and it can be dangerous depending on the concentration. That stuff hadn't been watered down yet, so it's very bad if it comes into contact with the skin or ingested. I don't want anyone getting hurt, and if there's someone sneaking in taking chemicals..."

A prickling started on the back of Elizabeth's neck. She tried to ignore it, but it left her with goosebumps. She tried not to squirm.

"You think someone stole stuff out of your classroom?"

"It's a possibility. But it's also possible that I didn't do a proper stock check, so I need to go back and check." Dominic shoved his hands into his pockets. "I hope that's the case and it's a mistake on my part. I shudder to think what someone can do with a bottle of hydrochloric acid that hasn't been watered down."

"I think I know," Elizabeth murmured. "A girl in my class got some thrown on her."

Dominic stared.

"What? She was assaulted?"

"She was lucky. It mostly hit her coat and skirt. I don't think she got any chemical burns, but she was rather shaken up by it. Her clothes did get ruined, though."

"Who would do that to a kid?"

Elizabeth sighed.

"I have no idea. They appeared out of nowhere, threw it on her, and ran off."

Dominic arched an eyebrow.

"And nobody caught them? We're in the middle of nowhere."

"You'd be surprised at how easy it is to disappear around here when you want to. I've done it plenty of times."

It was easy to hide anything if you had the inclination here. Elizabeth had done it plenty of times, and it made her feel powerful that she had a safe space that nobody knew about.

Dominic frowned, and then he turned away shaking his head.

"I will never understand people. Doing something so sense-less for no reason...it makes you wonder how twisted a mind is for being so cruel for something so stupid. If there is a reason at all."

"You've never wanted to hurt anyone, Dominic?"

Dominic stopped. For a moment, Elizabeth wondered if she was talking to a statue; she had never seen Dominic look so still. Then he turned back and gave her a tiny smile.

"I always want to hurt someone. But I have a conscience, so that's never going to happen. Unlike some people, I have self-control."

Elizabeth watched him walk away. Even though it had been an innocent enough comment, she felt like the science teacher had directed that last comment at her.

* * *

"I don't need to be in bed," Ellen protested as her daughter laid the duvet over her. "If I try to rest, I'm going to start remembering..."

"You were told to rest, Mom," Clara said, giving her a sharp look as she straightened up. "I know what you're like. You'll go for the bottle and drink it all down before you've taken a breath. That's not going to make things any better, you know."

Ellen scowled.

"I don't drink a whole bottle that quickly," she grumbled.

"You used to. I know you try to stick to one glass every now and then, but Dad said you had an entire bottle yesterday."

"With Lisa."

"Which doesn't make it any better, not when Lisa also drinks like a fish."

Ellen sat up.

"Clara, you may be a grown-up now, but I'm still your mother. Don't talk about my friend like that."

"And you need someone to get some sense into your head," Clara shot back. "Just do as you're told and get some sleep. I can get you some sleeping tablets, if you want..."

"No!"

This was frustrating to Ellen. She was still reeling from seeing what had happened to Miles, but she didn't want to be treated like a baby. As soon as she got home, she found her eldest child waiting for her. Clara had been distraught, and her clinging onto Ellen almost had her burst into tears. Miles had been one of Clara's favourite teachers, so to hear that he was dead had to have shaken her more than Ellen expected.

Clara sighed heavily and rubbed her hands over her face.

"Look, Mum, you've had a shock. Dad said you need to rest, something you didn't do yesterday."

"I thought I did."

"Then where did you go last night? Dad woke up and couldn't find you."

"He told you that."

"Of course he did! He's worried about you. That you might be slipping back..."

Ellen cut her off abruptly.

"Clara, there's nothing wrong with me other than suffering from shock. And I couldn't sleep last night, so I went for a walk. I went to the far end of the village and back again. The fresh air helped me sleep."

Her daughter looked like she didn't believe her, and that was frustrating. When Clara was a girl, she believed anything Ellen said. She was so innocent and smart. Unfortunately, the smart part of her was winning out over the innocent side, and Ellen didn't want that. Clara would figure out the truth sooner or later.

If she did, she would tell Jake and her brother. Then Ellen would be at fault for their family falling apart.

No, I will not be at fault. I never did anything wrong.

"Well, I'm going to be downstairs. Work allowed me to do it remotely today, so I'll stay here until Dad gets back tonight."

"You don't need to do that..."

"I do. I'm worried about you, Mum. Mark is as well, but he's not able to do anything from where he is. It's going to be a while before he can confirm her time off to join us."

Ellen didn't know what to say to that. Mark had moved to Canada to work as soon as he finished university in Cardiff, and he didn't often come back to visit. It would be amazing to see her younger child.

If only it weren't in these circumstances.

She managed a smile at her daughter.

"Thanks, darling. And I'm sorry. After what's happened..."

"You don't need to apologise." Clara leaned over and hugged Ellen. "You've found two bodies in such a short space of time, and they were friends. It's going to make anyone freak out. You're doing better than I would if I were in your position."

"I think you would be fine, Clara." Ellen kissed her cheek and eased back to look at the young woman. "You're tougher than I am. You would be able to cope."

"I don't know about that." Sighing, Clara straightened up. "Anyway, I'll be downstairs. Your phone and remote are beside you, so if you need anything just send me a text. I'll make lunch for us."

"Okay."

As long as she didn't go into the bathroom and look around for anything beyond a new roll of toilet paper, that was fine with Ellen.

As the door closed behind her, Ellen picked up the remote and turned on the TV. There were quite a few shows saved that she had been watching over the summer, but hadn't actually had the time. And the school summer holidays were two months long, so how had she not had time to binge-watch TV all day?

Maybe she needed to slow down at some point. Otherwise things were going to pass her by and Ellen would regret not doing everything before.

She settled on one of the shows, but it soon became clear that it wasn't going to work. The show was more convoluted than Ellen remembered, and it was something that her mind needed to completely focus on. Her thoughts would not settle, going back to what she saw at the school. Isabella and Miles' faces kept floating around, and Ellen felt like their eyes were still on her.

She couldn't begin to understand why anyone would do that, even if it was personal. She didn't want to think about how terrified Isabella must have felt when she was being held under the water, or how much pain Miles experienced.

It was like someone was torturing her friends, and then making it fate that Ellen was the one to find them. Ellen knew that was stupid to think, but it still felt like it.

Also, she couldn't stop thinking about Jane Christian. The little girl who had caused so much havoc with everything when she arrived. For nine months, she made life difficult. Bright girl, yes, and Ellen couldn't deny that she was talented. But she was a thorn in everyone's side. She was always getting into trouble.

It was no surprise that she ended up dead. It had been a question of when and not if. Although Ellen did feel a pang of guilt for what happened. That is not a way for a little girl to die.

Where were her family now? The last time Ellen saw them was the day they left the school. Jane's father had been furious, threatening Ellen before his wife pulled him away. There had been a threat of a lawsuit, but that had just been hot air. As far as Ellen was aware, nobody had asked her for compensation money. Jake said he had paid something, but he hadn't needed to. He just did it to stop the slander, hush money to make them go away. Ellen hated that he had needed to do that.

They were just angry and lashing out because they lost one of their children.

What if Jack Christian is the one who murdered Isabella and Miles? They did teach Jane...

Ellen knew she should leave it alone, but she knew that it would nag at her if she didn't find out. And her laptop was on the little desk under the window.

Clara didn't need to know...

Slipping out of bed, Ellen went over to the desk and picked up her laptop. If Clara came in and asked what she was doing, she could easily say she was trying to do some prep work. It still needed to be done despite not having access to her stuff at school. Settling back in bed, Ellen turned on her laptop and opened up the internet browser.

Now she paused. What did she even look for? Where did she go? Jack and Sophie Christian would be in their sixties by now. There was a chance that they had social media, but at the same time...

Might as well find out.

Ellen went onto Facebook, and typed in Sophie Christian's name. She was the more sociable one, so she was the more logical choice. And, sure enough, a profile with a picture of a woman who looked very similar to what Ellen had in her memory came up. She was smiling, looking like she had just finished running, wearing a medal with a number pinned to her top. Underneath was her job and location. Music teacher, Ilkeston. That was a town in Derbyshire.

That was her.

Ellen clicked on the profile, but found that the page was private outside of the basic information. No photos, no friends to look for, nothing. The only way she would be able to find out was to send Sophie a friend request. Given everything that had happened, that was not a good idea.

That was a dead end, and Jack Christian didn't even have Facebook.

Then she remembered. Jane had a couple of brothers. One was older and had been at university, so Ellen had never seen him, but she remembered the younger one. He had been in lower prep, away from the torment that his sister had gone through. A bright, talented boy, from what Ellen had heard. Very into his sports, much like Jane.

It took a moment for Ellen to remember his name, putting his name into Facebook. Sean Christian came up at the top result. Ellen clicked on the name, and stared at the cover photo. It had been over twenty years since she had last seen him as a nine-year-old boy, but it was Jane's brother. They looked so similar they could have passed for twins. He looked well, smiling for the camera. The cover photo was cropped, so there was an arm around his shoulders, keeping the focus on Sean.

His profile was locked down as well, much like his mother's. His location was Buxton, his occupation...logistics manager.

Ellen had never heard of the company, so she did a quick search. It was a company who controlled and moved explosives for the process of quarrying or in terms of defence. Not what she expected, but it was interesting.

How? Neither Isabella or Miles had been blown up. Nobody has.

Not yet, anyway.

The sound of her phone ringing distracted Ellen for a moment. Putting her laptop on the bed, she picked up her phone and slumped onto the pillows as she answered.

"Hello?"

"Hey, I heard what happened. God, I'm so sorry, Ellen."

Ellen sighed.

"Thanks, Lisa. I don't think it's really sunk in yet."

"Was it really that bad?"

"Do you need me to answer that?"

"I guess not." Lisa sounded troubled. "I can't believe this. First Isabella, and now Miles...is someone picking us off one by one?"

"I doubt that's the case, Lisa."

"What are the odds of it being something else, Ellen? They're both teachers here, and from what I heard, the same picture was found near the bodies."

Ellen stiffened.

"How did you hear about that?"

"You know that teachers gossip. Besides, one of the damn copies was shoved into my pigeon hole. Even with the 'you're next' message printed on the bottom."

Another one? Ellen had thought it was just a stupid prank, and they chose that photograph as a coincidence. Now it had been found at two murders, and people were beginning to receive them.

This was definitely linked. This had to be about Jane and what happened to her.

It's just a coincidence. That's all it is.

You can deny all you want. You know exactly what this is about.

"It's got to be about what happened," Lisa went on. "I can't see why anyone else would murder our friends, especially when they were killed so close together. It has to be..."

"Calm down, Lisa."

"How can I be calm? Two of my friends are dead. How can nobody be freaked with that?"

Ellen had to concur with that. She was rather uncomfortable about it as well. But she wasn't going to think about it like that. They had to think practically.

"I'm sure the police will be able to find out what's going on. It's their job, after all."

"I know, but..."

"We're not going to get mixed up in this, Lisa. You and I are going to be fine. The police will find the maniac, and then we'll be able to get our answers."

"What if they don't?" Lisa murmured.

She was beginning to make Ellen nervous, and that was not helpful. Ellen swallowed back her annoyance.

"They will. And then we'll be safe."

"I wish I had your confidence, Ellen."

"Why do you think I'm in charge?" Ellen looked at her paused TV, the images still up on the screen. "Have you spoken to Kerry? I haven't seen her since yesterday."

"I think she got the call before she left the house, so she's still there." Lisa's voice faltered. "You don't think..."

"Don't be silly. I'm sure she's fine." For once, Kerry's lateness worked for her. "Anyway, I've been told to rest, and I'll get told off by Clara if I don't."

"Nora is telling me I should distract myself, but that's easier said than done."

"We can but try."

Lisa took a deep breath, letting it out slowly.

"Okay. I'll try. But if anything else…"

"Nothing else is going to happen. We'll leave it to the police, okay?"

Ellen hung up before Lisa could respond, tossing her phone onto the bed and rubbing her fingers against her temples. That damn headache was not going away. If it turned into another migraine, she was going to be incapacitated for a while.

Maybe you should just take the…

No! I'm never taking those again. I don't need them.

Ellen closed her eyes and started to go through the medication her doctor had shown her. She was fine. She didn't need anything to make herself feel better. This was just a blip that was lowering her defences.

She was fine.

Chapter Ten

Miles was dead. Kerry let those words sink in. It didn't seem real. Miles would never have gotten himself into a position where he would end up being killed. He was too nice.

He always did as he was told. Was that the reason he was killed?

Kerry didn't want to speculate. It just made her think about things she shouldn't, and Kerry didn't want her mood to get even worse.

She entered the kitchen as her husband was making coffee. Sam looked up and raised his eyebrows at her outfit.

"You're a bit under-dressed for the school, aren't you? I didn't think you were allowed to wear your running gear unless there was a sporting event."

"I'm not going in today."

"Why not? Because you slept through the alarm and can't be bothered now?"

Kerry ignored her husband's quip. She took her water bottle over to the sink and unscrewed the cap.

"Miles is dead. They found his body this morning."

"What?" There was a clatter, and Kerry saw that Sam had almost dropped his mug. He put it firmly on the counter and mopped up the hot liquid that was staining the white countertop. "Are you serious? He's dead?"

"I'm afraid so. I don't know the details, but it was enough for Elizabeth's voice to be shaking." Kerry noticed that her hands were trembling as she filled up her water bottle, fumbling to turn the tap off. Water sloshed over her hand, and the cold made her flinch. "Anyway, we're to stay at home and do what work we can until the police say we can go back in."

"I'm surprised anyone can do work in these circumstances."

"We've got the kids coming in shortly after the bank holiday, and then there will be less time to get things ready." Kerry dried her hands and dried the water bottle before screwing the lid back on. "It's the joy of working at a boarding school."

Sam sighed and went over to the kitchen table.

"And I thought there had been enough tragedy at that place? I still remember that girl who was hit by a car..."

"That was over twenty years ago, Sam. Nothing like that has happened since."

"What about the abuse Isabella inflicted?"

Kerry stiffened.

"She didn't inflict any abuse. Those parents are just looking for a payout."

"You really believe that, do you?"

"You don't know Isabella, Sam. She would never hurt a child."

Sam snorted, taking a sip of his coffee.

"You know, there are a lot of rumours going around about the...punishments that the students get. Isabella Sanders is just the tip of the iceberg." He fixed her with a hard stare. "And you say you know nothing about it?"

Kerry hated it when her husband started being a lawyer around her. It was really annoying, and a little scary at times.

She glared back at him.

"I don't know anything," she said through gritted teeth. "And it has nothing to do with what is happening."

"Well, someone seems to think so."

"Leave your speculation for the courtroom, Sam. Don't use it on me." Kerry headed towards the door. "I'm going for a run, and then I'll get on with some work. Don't interrupt me."

"Likewise."

Kerry didn't respond as she left the house, closing the door a little too hard behind her. Then she slumped onto the steps as her legs trembled. Pressing the water bottle to her forehead, trying to cool her skin, she took a few deep breaths as she attempted to get back her composure. God, her husband was getting annoying. If he didn't bring in so much money, then Kerry wouldn't have given him the time of day. It certainly helped that he was very handsome as well; easier on the eye.

It was a shame that he was sharp, though. He didn't know about the Christian girl and what happened there, but he must have suspected. He had certainly treated her friends with a certain coolness that Kerry tried to play off as aloofness due to the nature of his job. In reality, he didn't like them. Especially Isabella. They had had many heated words in the past.

Did he suspect something? Kerry wondered if he knew, and he was holding onto it for a time when he could have a trump card. She had wondered that for years. Nothing had ever been said, but Sam's actions had made Kerry think when she was feeling a little vulnerable. It was the only reason she had stayed with him besides the money; Sam could turn everything upside-down if he knew what had happened.

Kerry didn't want that to happen. After all, she had only done as she was told. She was young and didn't want to argue. That would have ended up with her being ostracised as well.

If Sam knew the circumstances, he would understand.

Not wanting to think about that anymore, Kerry stood up slowly and headed towards the gate. She needed to have a run to clear her head, although she had a feeling it was going to be a while before that happened.

* * *

Ellen waited until she was sure Clara was deep in her work before she tiptoed downstairs. From personal experience, she knew that her daughter didn't notice anything around her once she was engrossed in whatever she was doing. She wouldn't notice that her mother had slipped out of the house.

She needed a walk to clear her head. It was not happening when she was lying in bed trying to watch TV. Not when thoughts of Jane were still in her head, and they were refusing to leave. Fresh air was what she needed, although it was very warm and she would more than likely end up being sweaty and out of breath.

Maybe she should get back into some exercise. It had been a while since Ellen had done anything sporty unless it was part of a school activity. She was gifted with a slim figure, but that was about it. She didn't have the fitness to go along with it.

Miles hadn't minded. He said you looked great no matter what.

Ellen swiped that from her mind. She didn't not want to think about that.

Sure enough, when she got to the bottom of the stairs, Ellen saw her daughter's back as she sat at the dining table. She didn't turn around, which made Ellen feel sure that Clara had her airpods in, and the music would be blasting. How she wasn't deaf at her age was anyone's guess.

Picking up her trainers, Ellen slipped them on, putting her keys into her pocket. After a moment's debate, she left her phone on the hall dresser. She didn't want to have it on her and then Clara or Jake would be able to contact her. They wouldn't be happy that she left without warning, but Ellen didn't care.

She needed to do this.

It felt like a relief stepping outside. Even with the hot sun, there was a cool breeze that made it bearable. It made the hem of her skirt ripple and tickle her chest. That felt better than earlier in the day.

Ellen closed the door as quietly as she could and then set off down the road, heading away from the nearest exit from her house. If she went that way, she would have to pass the window, and there would be a chance that Clara would see her. Her daughter was really concerned about her, and while Ellen appreciated it she didn't want to have her girl hovering around her.

Maybe later when she had found a way to relax.

It took a while to go past the other houses and out onto the road on the far side, which made Ellen glad she had put on her trainers.

If only she had brought her water bottle, or her wallet. She was probably going to get thirsty. Oh, well. Lisa didn't live far away. She and Nora would let her have something to drink if Ellen passed that way. Someone would look after her if she asked.

Then someone caught Ellen's eye. A woman jogging along the opposite pavement, covering the ground with a smooth, elegant stride that made it look really easy. Her shorts and black vest were a stark contrast to her bright orange trainers, a water bottle in one hand with her phone strapped into the band on her arm, a black headband keeping her hair out of her face.

It took a moment for Ellen to recognise her. She hadn't seen Leanne Durose like this before. Not with that look of concentration on her face. She waved.

"Leanne!"

Leanne glanced over, only to do a double-take and slow down. She stared at Ellen for a moment before shaking herself and jogging across the road, giving Ellen her usual beaming smile.

"Hey, Ellen," she shouted. Then she pulled out one of her airpods as she slowed to a stop, her voice going back down to a normal volume. "Sorry, I had my music on really loudly. I tend to forget that."

"Indeed," Ellen murmured.

She knew all about that. Leanne seemed to have no volume button. It worked to get the kids under control, but it also meant she forgot to speak normally around other people for a while afterwards.

"How are you doing?" Leanne asked, peering at her. "I heard you found Miles. I'm so sorry."

"How did you know that?"

"David told me."

Ellen arched an eyebrow. Of course David would tell Leanne. The two of them seemed to have a bond that nobody could understand. There was speculation that David and Leanne were having an affair, and Ellen was inclined to believe it. That would break Elizabeth's heart if she knew, though.

"I see."

Leanne shrugged.

"He does tell me things when I ask. We're friends, after all, and he is the acting head now."

"Hmm." Ellen looked Leanne up and down. "I wish I could run like you. I don't think my knees can cope with it now."

Leanne laughed.

"I'm sure you'll do better than me. Didn't you used to do cross-country when you were my age?"

"That was a long time ago."

"Bullshit. I look at you, and you look young and fresh." Leanne gestured at herself. "I hope I can look as good as you when I'm your age."

Ellen smiled.

"You know how to flatter people, Leanne."

"Only when it's true," Leanne said brightly. She took a swig of water. "I've got to get on with my workout, so do you want to walk with me for a little bit? I presume you're trying to get some air."

"Absolutely." Ellen fell into step beside the younger woman. "My husband and daughter are really worried about me. They keep saying that I need to rest and let them do everything, but every time I sit down and stay still, I keep remembering...well... stuff I don't want to remember."

Leanne looked sympathetic.

"They just want to be sure you're not going to go into shock or break down. It's a normal reaction after such an event."

"I'm tougher than that. I wish they would stop treating me like spun glass." Ellen shook her head. "I love them, but it can be stifling. I'm sure you felt the same way with George's father."

"Not really." Leanne's voice faltered. "We...we were actually great. He was like a prince, and he treated me like his princess."

Ellen didn't know what to say to that. Leanne had arrived a year ago, her son one of the students while she took on the music teacher post. She had mentioned that her husband had died of cancer, and she had been looking to make a fresh start elsewhere. The students loved her, and quite a few of the male teachers had no problem giving her a second glance when she was in the room. She was so young and bubbly compared to Ellen.

She was sure that would change after she had been at Wolsey Prep a little longer as an adult. Leanne was malleable, but she could still break.

"Where's George, anyway? Didn't you say he was with his dad's parents?"

"Yes. They're in the Lake District. I asked if they could take him on a holiday so he wasn't stuck at home with me." Leanne gestured at their surroundings. "This place is gorgeous, but there's nothing to do for a growing boy. You raised your children, so I'm sure you know what I mean."

"I do. Clara and Mark begged me to take them to other clubs despite having been at school all day and coming home at five. Especially during the holidays. Neither of them liked being stuck at home."

Leanne laughed.

"I was pretty much the same when I was a kid. Mum and Dad told me not to, but my sister and I would sneak out of the house and explore. You would be surprised at what we found."

Sneak out of the house and explore. Ellen had almost forgotten.

"You used to live in the old master's house, didn't you? Until your parents got divorced and you left with your mum."

"We did. It was actually a pretty cool house. Our rooms were decorated to how we wanted them. It was close to school so we didn't have to worry about rushing to school and if we forgot something we could rush back without any problems. And I did love our garden." Leanne sighed. "I wish we could've taken the house with us, but you can't do that unfortunately."

Ellen watched Leanne thoughtfully. She remembered when she first met Leanne Durose. She had been seven years old, quite small for her age and really shy. Her older sister was very protective of her.

Speaking of which...

"Do you remember Jane Christian, Leanne?"

Leanne blinked.

"You what? That's a name from the past!"

"You recall her, though, don't you?"

"Of course I do. My sister and Jane were good friends. Probably Jane's only friend. Everyone else chose to keep their distance because she was a target." Leanne's jovial expression faded and she frowned. "I never understood why kids can be so cruel until I became a teacher. It was...what those children did to Jane was just horrific. Bonnie said that she and Jane would escape into the grounds and hide, just to get away from everything."

"They missed a few lessons doing that."

"I think having detention to escape the bullies was worth it. Kept them away from the little shits." Leanne scoffed. "It didn't help in the end, did it? Jane still ended up dead. I wouldn't be surprised if one of those brats chased her out in front of that car."

Ellen didn't know what to say to that. An image of Jane's broken body flashed in her mind, and she pushed it away. Not what she wanted right now.

"I take it David's told you about the pictures of Jane turning up next to the bodies?" she asked. "You two seem to talk about everything."

"Yes, he told me. And I remember the one pinned up on the corkboard." Leanne peered at Ellen. "Do you think this is about Jane? That someone might be trying to get their revenge for what happened to her?"

"I honestly don't know. After all, I know Isabella and Miles didn't hurt her."

They didn't need to, did they?

"Even then," Ellen went on, concentrating on the woman before her, "it's been over twenty years. Why is it happening now? If it was about Jane and what happened to her, why would they wait all this time?"

"Maybe they didn't know."

"What do you mean?"

Leanne shrugged.

"There's a possibility that nobody knew the truth about what happened. I mean, the rumours at the time were pretty basic, and they weren't disclosed to the public. Then someone might have come across something that said what truly happened, and they got angry about it."

"Like who?"

"Maybe a family member. Maybe someone close to Jane. It could even be another teacher who felt guilty for not doing something back then. There could be a multitude of reasons." Leanne took a swig of her water, wiping her mouth with the back of her hand. "I'm just talking out of my butt here. Sometimes, people don't need a reason and just suddenly do it. They could be off their medications, for all we know, and are suffering from delusions."

"From what I've seen, if the killer was deluded they're still in control of their assets," Ellen said quietly. She absently tapped her fingers against her keys through the fabric of her pocket. "If that's the case, that's quite scary. I wouldn't want that guy after me."

"It could be a woman," Leanne pointed out. "Women are just as capable of murder, maybe even more so."

There was that, which didn't make Ellen feel any better. Her mouth was getting dry, and she eyed Leanne's water bottle, hoping that she would be offered some. Instead Leanne seemed to shift and move the hand holding the bottle away.

"I suppose we're never going to know," Leanne went on. "I don't think I'll understand what goes on in someone's head to do something so awful."

That felt loaded with meaning, but Ellen's headache was coming back again, and she wasn't too sure. She was probably going to read between the lines something that wasn't there if she wasn't careful.

"Maybe Bonnie would have an idea."

"Bonnie?"

"Well, she was Jane's friend, wasn't she? I think she might have some clues as to who might be doing this if it is connected to what happened to Jane." Ellen regarded Leanne, who's expression was shifting. "Perhaps you could ask her?"

"Bonnie's dead."

The words felt like a slap in the face. Ellen wasn't sure she had heard correctly.

"What? She's dead? When did that happen?"

"Two years ago. She's been having problems with her mental health for years. Mostly due to bullying at school, which badly affected her." Leanne took another gulp of water, her expression now blank. "She overdosed, not able to take it anymore. I found her body."

"Oh."

Ellen hadn't expected that. She did recall Bonnie being a sensitive little girl who burst into tears if something didn't happen as she wanted, but she had been a smart and tenacious kid. Very loyal. And now she was dead?

Ellen didn't know what to say after that?

"If you'll excuse me, Ellen, I need to finish my run." Leanne adjusted her headband. "I've got a lot to do, and I don't want to deviate too much from my to-do list."

"Leanne, I'm sorry..."

But Leanne had already run off, crossing the road and settling into her rhythm again, her trainers slapping at a regular pace on the tarmac. Although Ellen could see the tension in her shoulders as the younger woman moved away.

She had hit a nerve. Ellen hadn't realised that Bonnie Durose was dead. Elizabeth had mentioned running into her in London, but that must have been before she took her own life. It was a surprise that Ellen hadn't heard about it.

Her headache was still pounding, and Ellen remembered that she hadn't managed to get a drink from Leanne's bottle. Damn, if only she had brought her wallet with her.

But the pub let people have a glass of water for free. Maybe she should try there. Resolved, Ellen set off again, her mind turning over what Leanne had told her about Bonnie, and what she had said about who might have killed her friends.

This was going to make her headache even worse.

Chapter Eleven

The run didn't make Kerry feel any better. If anything, it just made the thoughts in her head spin even more, and they were now stuck on repeat. Kerry felt like she was being driven insane.

This whole thing was a mess. Everything was going to shit. Kerry had thought everything was going really well, that they were having good fun and there was a nice rhythm going with the kids and the fellow teachers. Kerry didn't think she could ask for a better life.

It all started coming apart when Isabella was arrested for assault. She never said a word, always denying everything, and Kerry didn't know how to feel about that. It was almost like Isabella was keeping a trump card, just in case something happened that required to gain the upper hand. Vicious as she was with her actions, Isabella was wily. She knew when she needed to keep something back.

She could blow the lid off the whole thing. Then there would be more jobs in jeopardy.

If you didn't want to be in this position, you should have stood up for yourself. Now you're stuck.

What if the police think I killed her because she knew too much?

That thought had sobered Kerry up. What if someone else had murdered Isabella because of what she knew? She had been talking about not going down without a fight when Kerry last saw her. Did that mean she was going to speak up about what really goes on?

No, that wouldn't happen. Ellen would deal with it. She knew how to get everyone to calm down and see reason. She was a good leader.

She's not a good leader if someone died in her care.

By the time Kerry returned home, she was feeling mentally drained. Her body ached, but her mind was exhausted. Her hands trembling, she let herself into the house.

"Sam, I'm back!" She kicked off her trainers, not hearing a response. "Sam?"

He was probably focused on his work. He did get engrossed, especially when it was intense. Padding softly across the floor, Kerry entered the kitchen, only to find Sam putting his laptop away and zipping up the bag.

"You've finished already?"

"I'm afraid not. I've just had a call from my boss." Sam sighed as he put some folders into the side pocket of his bag. "I need to go to Cambridge."

Kerry frowned.

"What? Now? You never said anything about it before."

"This came in last minute. We've got a negotiation to do, and the guy who was going to do it ended up getting sick. As I've been working on it with him, I have to take his place." Sam gave her an apologetic smile. "Sorry, Kerry, but I have to go."

"But it's Friday. Can't you wait until Monday to go? Or Sunday night?"

"It's taking place tomorrow. Don't look at me like that," Sam went on as Kerry stared at him, "it can happen sometimes. And if Saturday's the only time the client can get off, we're going to have to go along with it."

Kerry didn't like it. Much as she preferred having a quiet house, she didn't want Sam to leave her right now. Not when her friends were getting killed. If anything, Kerry felt paranoid.

"Can't I persuade you to stay?" she asked.

Sam blinked at her.

"You want me to stay?"

"Well, after everything that's happened..."

"Oh, Kerry." Sam approached her, and put his arms around her. "I know you're uncomfortable with everything, and given the circumstances I understand. But I need to do this. It's more money for us, and I get a cut of the fee afterwards."

"Even so..."

"Just one night. That's all. And I'll be back as soon as I can." Sam kissed her forehead. "Why don't you go and stay with one of your friends if you're nervous about being alone? Give Ellen a call and ask if you can stay in one of her rooms."

"I thought you didn't like Ellen."

"I don't, but that doesn't mean I can stop you if you want some company. And I'm sure Ellen needs someone with her right now if she's the one finding all the bodies."

Kerry didn't answer that. She could have pointed out that Ellen had her husband, but then she knew that would be a lie. Jake loved his wife, but Ellen's feelings had never stayed the same. Kerry wouldn't be surprised if her friend said that she only married Jake because of his standing and connections rather than how he made her feel.

Kerry liked Ellen, but she was ruthless and methodical. Even when it came to her marriage.

"I might just do that," she murmured. "She's going to need a friend. I can't imagine how she felt finding Miles after finding

Isabella."

"She was close to Miles, wasn't she?"

"It depends on how you define 'close', but yes, they were."

Sam didn't answer. He simply kissed her head again and picked up his laptop case, slinging it over his shoulder as he grabbed onto the gym bag by his feet.

"Anyway, I'll be back as soon as I can. Just make sure you lock all of the doors."

"You don't think someone's going to come after me?" Kerry asked, feeling a cold chill down her back. The killer wasn't going to come after her as well, was he?

If it's about that Christian girl, then there's a good chance...

"I doubt it, but I don't want to take any chances. So if you're not going out, lock all of the doors. If you want to stay with someone, just let me know so I'm not panicking when I come back tomorrow."

Tomorrow. That felt like a very long way away, and Kerry wasn't sure how she felt about it. She put her water bottle in the sink and absently wiped her sweaty hands on her jacket.

"Okay. Fine. I'll see if one of the girls will let me stay. Once I've had a bath and cleaned myself up."

"Okay. Text me when you are settled." Sam approached her and kissed her cheek. "I'm sure you'll be fine, though. Whoever did this is going to be caught. Trust me."

Kerry didn't respond. She wasn't entirely sure about that. And there was also that feeling in her gut that whoever murdered Isabella and Giles wasn't done.

Which meant she could be a target as well.

She didn't move until she heard the front door closing as her husband left. Then she slumped against the sink. God, what was she thinking? Why didn't she beg for Sam to stay? Given everything going on, it felt better having someone at home with her. With her husband at home, Kerry had the chance of being distracted, even just for a little bit. But with him gone, all she was going to think about was...*that* day.

Or, rather, that nine-month period that culminated in a death. One that shook Kerry despite her feelings on the matter.

Pushing herself off the sink, Kerry made her way upstairs, scrolling through her phone until she found the number she wanted. Leanne picked up on the third ring, sounding breathless.

"Hey, Kerry. What's up?"

"What on earth are you up to?"

"I was having my daily run. I've just run to Earl Soham and I'm on my way back."

Shit. That was at least two-and-a-half miles away. To do that both ways...Kerry couldn't even do two miles in one go, jogging in a large circle. And she used to do marathons. Even then, she hadn't been able to run it all from start to finish.

"How the fuck do you manage to run that much? I can't do that, and I like to think I'm a decent runner."

"I go on park runs whenever I can. A five-mile run is nothing." Leanne's breathing sounded a little less laboured now. "What's up? Things okay?"

"Sam's suddenly gone to Cambridge, and he's going to be staying overnight." Kerry went into the bathroom and turned the taps on. "I'm not feeling comfortable about staying here alone, not with everything going on. Can I stay with you?"

There was a moment's hesitation, and then Leanne was speaking brightly.

"Oh, okay. Although I thought you'd ask Ellen or Lisa."

Kerry didn't immediately answer, tucking her phone between

her ear and shoulder as she picked out the bubble bath and tipped a generous amount into the tub.

"Well, they have their partners with them, whereas you and I are going to be on our own. We should stick together in pairs. Your son is still on holiday, isn't he?""

"Sounds like an idea," Leanne chirped. "If I'm honest, I was feeling uncomfortable about being alone. I can't sit still thinking about what could happen next."

"Since when have you ever sat still? You've never done that since you were one of my students."

"Fair point. Anyway, it's going to take me a while to get back home. What time were you thinking?"

"I was going to have a bath and pack my things. I'll text you when I'm about to head off." Kerry put the bubble bath down and headed into the bedroom. "Thanks for this, Leanne. I appreciate it."

"We have to stick together, don't we? I'm sure they'll find the sick bastard."

"I hope so," Kerry murmured. She sat on the bed and took off her socks. "Thanks again. I'll text you later."

"Okay. Let me know if you have a change of plans as well. It's no biggie, and it will save me worrying."

"Will do."

Kerry hung up and tossed her phone onto the bed. Normally, she wouldn't be asking her former student and now her colleague if she could stay with her, but there was an ulterior motive. Leanne's sister had been friends with Jane Christian, and she seemed to be the link. Kerry had every intention of grilling Leanne until she got her answers.

Leanne wouldn't be bubbly after she was done with her. Especially if she knew anything.

Invigorated knowing that she had some purpose going for-ward, Kerry stripped off and headed into the bathroom. Once the bath was full enough, she turned the taps off and sank into the water. It felt like it was burning, and it made her wince, but it did feel good. Normally, Kerry would have a shower after running, but she had time now to have a bath. She could take her time and form a plan on how to extract information from Leanne.

This was going to be something new. Ellen was the one who was good at getting information she wanted; if it was her, she could get Leanne to squeal. Kerry was going to have to remember her techniques.

She wondered how Ellen was getting on. She had found both bodies, and she was still able to stand upright. It was a wonder how the older woman wasn't crumbling to pieces. Maybe she was, but once nobody was looking. Ellen Lawson was tough.

Hopefully, her mental health wasn't going to take a dive again. Kerry remembered when Ellen was having issues a few years back, shortly after the...incident. She went from being depressed and having no energy to running around like she was the energizer bunny. It had been there before the incident happened, but somehow it became more pronounced. In recent years, Ellen's health seemed to have improved, and she was pretty much her normal self.

Although Kerry did wonder if Ellen had taken a dip again. She had been a little manic, never seeming to sit down and looking like she was staring at something but there was no one there. Coming back to get everything ready for the new term had shown that Ellen seemed to be a little better, but Kerry had seen the agitated way her friend tapped her fingers on her knee, or how she kept darting her gaze around the room. She didn't even seem to realise that she was doing it.

It could be stress at finding a dead body. Or maybe...

It's nothing to do with you. Ellen told you that when you helped her pick up the items that had fallen out of her bag. Leave it to her family to deal with it.

I just hope she doesn't do something stupid.

As Kerry washed herself, sinking into the blissful water, she became absorbed in her thoughts. It was no coincidence that Jane Christian's picture was left around the school. It had to be about her. But none of them killed her. She got hit by a car, and nobody owned up to it. It was just an accident on a busy day, that was all.

Also, it was over twenty years ago. Why make a move on it now? Surely too much time had passed to make things right.

Jane almost drowned in the pool, and she was attacked in the workshop. That is how Isabella and Miles died. If I'm on the list, how am I going to die?

A memory flitted across Kerry's mind, but she pushed it away. No, that was not going to happen. She would fight before that happened. If she was going to become another target, they were not going to have it easy. Kerry would make sure they came away with worse than she received.

Nobody was going to get the drop on her.

Finally, Kerry got out of the bath and wrapped herself in one of her towels. Now she was feeling a little better. She was clean, and she had a general idea of how to get Leanne to tell her what she knew. If she didn't know what was going on, she would have contact details for her sister. Bonnie had to be behind this. Kerry would not be surprised if Bonnie's name came up.

She entered her bedroom, only to stop in the doorway. Something didn't seem right. But on a cursory glance, nothing was out of place. Not that Kerry could see. And yet she couldn't help but think that something was wrong.

Oh, shit. Someone was in the house.

Kerry barely had time to turn around before she felt a hand press on the side of her head and slam it into the doorway.

* * *

Her body felt like it had goosebumps all over. And her head felt as if someone had stuck it in a vice. Kerry didn't think she had felt worse after an intense night of drinking.

Then she realised that she couldn't open her eyes. They just wouldn't move, and forcing it just hurt. The area around her eyes was throbbing, but when Kerry tried to move her hands so she could feel what was going on, they wouldn't move, either. They were held together above her head, and something smooth but tight was wrapped around her wrists. It took her a moment to figure out that her legs were tied together as well.

She had been bound naked on the bed and held in place by the bars on her bed. And she couldn't see.

Shit.

Panicking, Kerry began to scream. Her neighbours weren't that far away, they had to hear something.

"Help! Somebody! He...!"

Pain exploded in her face as something solid slammed into her, knocking her back into the pillows and making her teeth rattle. Then she tasted blood. She had bitten her tongue.

Kerry turned her head to spit the blood out. Then she heard a voice coming from the side of the bed.

"You can scream all you want. Your neighbours are still on holiday. Nobody's coming to help you."

Kerry froze. That voice. She knew it.

Oh, God. It was...

"I don't want you to talk. I want you to listen." There was a clink of glass on the bedside table. "Because you can't see, I want you to know what's going to happen to you."

"Please..." Kerry whispered, panic gripping her chest. "Why are you doing this? Just..."

More pain exploded in her face, and then something in her nose went crack. Shit, her nose was broken.

"I told you that you weren't to talk. Speak again, and you'll be gagged. Do you want that?"

Terrified, Kerry shook her head. What was going on? How had she not seen this coming?

"I'm guessing you're thinking why am I doing this, but I think I can give you a clue. March 2001. A girl gets acid thrown on her by another girl in your presence. She ends up with a chemical burn on her hand, and the police get involved. Which, of course, they should have been, seeing as a child had been the victim of an acid attack."

Kerry had been finding it hard to breathe due to her nose, but now it was getting harder. Shit, it really was about her.

"Despite her statement that she knew who it was, and that you were there, you lied and said you never saw who threw the acid on her. You gave the bitch an alibi and made the girl suffer. The police couldn't do anything about it, so everyone got away with it. Nobody got punished, except for the victim. Didn't she get detention for lying about a teacher?"

Kerry's mouth was dry. She licked her lips and tried to gulp in air. God, she was going to have a heart attack in a minute.

"I don't see how that's fair. The victim gets into trouble for trying to get people to listen. Just disgusting. That's why I glued your eyes shut. Because you witnessed a horrific crime, and you didn't do anything. Like Miles Sims' mouth was glued, because he said nothing. Because he was too busy drooling over a married woman." Disdain dripped and seemed to hang in the air. "I know why you all did it. Who started this, and why. All for a pathetic reason. And you let a volatile child take it several steps too far with her bullying."

Kerry could feel her tears clogging her throat. She wanted to cry, but she couldn't; she was too scared to do it in case she was punched again. Then the sound of clinking glasses and liquid being poured drew her attention.

"You knew, and you didn't say that you weren't going to bully a little girl. She was twelve. She never did anything to you. Now she's dead, and you haven't suffered the consequences. I'm sure if you were reported to the police, all of you would band together. Besides, this is far more satisfying to me. I get to see you suffer just as Jane Christian did."

But why? Kerry wanted to ask why this was happening. Why now? But her dry lips were too stiff to move, fear keeping her silent.

"So, because you can't see, I'm going to tell you what is going to happen." She could hear the swirl of the liquid. "The teacher's pet threw hydrochloric acid onto Jane Christian. She was lucky to get away with a burn on her arm, and you said you saw nothing. So, that's what's going to happen to you. You're going to be burned with acid, and you are not going to see a thing." Dropping to a whisper: "But you'll feel everything. More than Jane ever did. And you'll deserve it."

Kerry's panic was building so fast she could hardly breathe. She tried to get away, but she couldn't get out of her bindings. They were secure, and they weren't budging. Not being able to see just made everything worse.

Oh, God. Not this. Please, don't...

She felt her stomach contract when a cool substance dripped onto her belly. For a split second, it stayed cold, and then it began to itch, followed by an intense burn that made her gasp. Kerry wriggled, and she felt the acid trickle across her belly and drip off her as she turned to the side. That felt even worse than the initial contact.

Then more was dropped onto her, dotted about her belly. She couldn't get away, and the burning sensation was getting worse. Kerry gritted her teeth, trying not to scream. Maybe if she didn't scream, she would be let go. Maybe she wouldn't get killed.

Who was she kidding? This was how she was going to die.

Kerry couldn't stop herself from screaming as more was thrown on her legs. Now it felt as if she had been rolled into a fire. She wanted to kick and scream, and her legs refused to move. She couldn't kick off whatever was keeping them pinned together.

The smell of burning flesh reached her nostrils, and Kerry felt sick. Oh, God, she was going to throw up. Turning her head, Kerry retched, feeling the bile burning her stomach.

This couldn't be happening. She was going to wake up and find herself still in the bath. This was not actually happening to her.

Reality slammed into her as the acid was splashed across her chest, excruciating pain making her shriek as it melted onto her nipples. The burning was all over, and Kerry felt like she was having a seizure as her whole body shook. Her head was spinning, her stomach heaving and her heart raced so fast Kerry was sure she would pass out.

"I'm going to make you burn," she managed to snarl, some-how finding her voice. "I'm going to make sure you burn in hell."

A chuckle somewhere above her made her freeze. It was so cold she didn't recognise the person anymore.

"I think you'll be burning long before I do. Even if you survive, you won't be able to tell the police anything." Then a leathery hand grabbed at her face, keeping her head still. "Now, open wide. I think you need a drink."

Kerry barely had time to scream before the burning sensation hit her in the back of the throat.

Chapter Twelve

Wednesday 7th March 2001

They are going too far. I can't believe how brazen PB is. Nothing seems to stop her if QB tells her to keep going.

Now she's stolen acid from the science room and thrown it at J as she was waiting to go home. Most of it got on her coat and bag, but some got on her hand and arm. Apparently, she was screaming when Miss M found her. Even then, she told J to stop behaving like a baby.

She's a child. Why are they targeting her? What did she do to any of them? I've asked Mum about it before, and she admits that she doesn't know. She thinks it's just a squabble between the students and it's getting out of hand, but even she can't get the head to listen. She doesn't approve, but she can't do anything.

It's why I haven't been targeted myself. Mum knows better than to stand up to QB. J only has me on her side, and she begged me not to tell her parents. She knows how much her dad's job means to him, and she doesn't want to ruin it for him. But she keeps telling me that she wants to go back home. It's hell for her, and the thought of this happening to anyone else in her family scares her.

I saw her brother today. He was angry that nobody is standing up for J except for me. Mum and Dad still don't know the full extent.

I do. J does. And so does her brother.

He hates that he can't be there for his sister. He wants to tell their parents, but J doesn't think they'll leave even with this. They're desperately trying to fit in. Even though QB ignores J's Mum when they're in the same room.

I think they should tell. Ever since J arrived she's been a target, and it's not fair to her. J's brother said anyone who targets a child through no fault of their own are the worst. I agree.

Like Miss M. She had to have seen PB, and she still thought J was overreacting. Now J is going to have a permanent scar on her arm because she wouldn't give her immediate first aid. J won't be able to swim for some time until she's properly healed.

We have to say something. I'm scared that my friend is going to end up dead if this carries on.

* * *

Elizabeth sat on the wall and looked at the farm further down the hill. It looked like the farmer was up, getting everything sorted for the day. She didn't think she would be able to cope with waking up that early.

Then again, she was probably going to end up waking up early tomorrow. Once she got home, Elizabeth had tried to distract herself and had ended up falling asleep on the sofa watching TV. Only to be plagued by horrible dreams. Memories of what happened years ago kept coming back, and she had ended up in a nightmare running away from a faceless killer who was threatening to kill her. Normally, she would be telling herself that it was a stupid dream, and she could put it to one side.

Only this felt more real. And after what happened to Isabella and Miles, Elizabeth's mind had been going haywire. She liked to think that she didn't have an overactive imagination, and it was happening now. She hated it.

Going for a walk had meant to be something to forget the nightmares, but it wasn't working. Now she was sitting in the middle of a field, wondering what the hell was going to happen next.

Knowing that there was someone out there who had killed twice left her feeling cold. Were they watching the others? Were they being stalked? It felt like there were eyes on her back, but whenever Elizabeth looked around there was nobody there.

God, she was turning into a nervous wreck. She would end up like Ellen on medication if she wasn't careful. Ellen wouldn't admit it to anyone that she was taking tablets, but Elizabeth had caught her a few times. She never said a word, knowing that Ellen wanted privacy and she respected that. Then again, she hadn't seen Ellen take any lately, so maybe whatever had happened was better, and she didn't need to take medication anymore.

Ellen Lawson was a strong woman. She knew how to keep her head high. Elizabeth was falling apart already. She wasn't feeling very strong right now.

A car coming along the farm path caught Elizabeth's eye. She watched it pull up outside the little cottage on the outskirts of the farmyard, the neatness of the garden and fresh, clean state of the cottage making it look like it was in a completely different world. Her heart missed a beat as David got out and waved at the farmer, who was leaving the yard with his dog. The older man waved back, and words floated up to Elizabeth, too far away for her to know what was being said.

As the farmer walked away, Elizabeth got off the wall and made her way down the slope. David looked like he had been out running, wearing shorts and trainers with a t-shirt that seemed to stick to his body with sweat. It wasn't the first time Elizabeth had seen him like this, but this time Elizabeth was able to ogle him without wondering if anyone could see her.

Somehow, his shoulders looked a little wider in just a t-shirt. And those legs were more muscular than she recalled. As she got closer, Elizabeth wondered what David would say if she asked to see more of him. Preferably with no clothes on.

No, of course she couldn't ask that. He was, essentially, her boss. That was inappropriate.

Such a shame...

David turned as Elizabeth reached the fence, blinking in surprise when he saw her.

"Elizabeth? What are you doing out here?"

"I was restless, so I went out for a walk." Elizabeth tried not to lick her lips as she looked David up and down. "Where have you been? I thought you would be at the school a bit longer."

"The police told everyone that we needed to vacate so they could process the area, so I went up to the college to have a meeting with Jake Lawson." David took off his glasses and used the bottom of his t-shirt to wipe his face. "We then went for a jog around the grounds. For a man in his sixties, he's very energetic."

Elizabeth's response had vanished when she saw the bare skin under his shirt for the first time. Damn, he was ripped. How was he in his forties and looked this good? It felt like someone was teasing her with a guy she couldn't touch.

"Elizabeth?"

"Huh?"

Elizabeth blinked. David was now looking at her oddly, adjusting his glasses. Feeling her face getting warm, Elizabeth cleared her throat.

"Sorry. I guess...I'm just a little...out of sorts."

David gave her a smile that made Elizabeth feel weak at the knees.

"You're not the only one. We're all rather out of sorts. Do you want to come inside?"

"What?"

"It's not that difficult. Do you want to come inside? We might as well have a coffee or something. Then I'll drive you home, if you want."

"I...thanks."

Was this actually happening? Was she going into David's home? In the two years since he had arrived, he hadn't invited anyone into his home. Elizabeth could just about see it from the school, and she had wondered what it was like inside. Now he was actually allowing her to join him?

Her stomach felt like it was housing butterflies as she managed a smile.

"Okay. That's kind of you."

"I do my best." David beckoned her to follow him. "Come on in."

Elizabeth followed him inside, and looked around. It was quite a quaint little home. Rustic, very clean. Very cosy, in fact. Not what Elizabeth had been expecting. The living room was small but surprisingly spacious, a large TV fixed onto the wall and a large grey L-shaped sofa against two walls. A desk was by a floor-to-ceiling bookcase, settled under the window with a perfect view of Wolsey Prep just down the hill.

Elizabeth looked at the books on the shelf. A couple of autobiographies of footballers, some historical textbooks, and a few true crime stories. If she didn't know that a guy lived here alone, she did now.

"Let's go into the kitchen," David said as he left the room. "We can talk while the kettle's boiling. Oh, shit." He winced at the sight of the neatly folded pile of clothes on the kitchen table. "Sorry, I forgot about that."

"We all forget," Elizabeth assured him.

She wasn't about to say that she didn't really put her washing away. It got washed, dried, and never made its way back into their drawers. This was nothing compared to her home.

"I definitely need a shower." David took off his t-shirt and opened the washing machine, tossing it inside. "That can wait, if you don't mind me looking like a sweaty mess."

"I...I don't mind."

Elizabeth was sure her eyes were going to pop out of her head, unable to stop her gaze raking over David's body. It was like he was soft and hard in the right places, smooth and glistening in sweat. Elizabeth's fingers itched to reach out and touch him, to follow the muscles down to his waistband, and maybe below.

She wondered if he would change out of his shorts as well; she certainly wouldn't object.

"Do you go running, Elizabeth?" David's voice made her jump. "I heard you were quite athletic when you were younger."

"Oh. You did?" Elizabeth squeaked. She gulped when David arched an eyebrow at her. "Well, I was pretty good at running, but I haven't done much lately. I've just been too busy being an adult to work out."

"You do surprise me." David looked her up and down. "From the look of it, you seem to keep yourself in shape. You can't say that is from sitting behind a desk."

Was he checking her out? Elizabeth shoved her hands into

her pockets. If she didn't, she was going to give in to the urge to touch him.

"I do a lot of walking around the school. You end up doing a lot of steps that way, as I'm sure you know."

David tilted his head to one side as he regarded her. Now he was making Elizabeth want to squirm. Why wasn't he putting another shirt on? It was like he knew how he was affecting her and was teasing her.

He was one for teasing, but this seemed to have shifted.

The kettle chose that moment to announce that it had boiled, and David turned away, getting mugs out of the cupboard. His backside looked taut under his shorts, and Elizabeth had to look elsewhere to stop herself from staring like a silly little girl. She went over to the window and looked out. From this side, she could see the pigs in the pigsty, just out of sight around the wall. She could hear the snoring of the large animals, and the stench wafted past her nose, even with the window shut.

"How can you live this close to a farm and not notice the smell?" she asked. "What made you pick this place?"

"I had to find somewhere in a hurry, and this place was available." There was a clink of ceramic behind her. "I'm not fussy, so I took it. And the cottage is comfortable, so it makes up for the smell and the occasional noise."

"Somewhere in a hurry?"

"I was looking for something different, and I saw the job advert on the last day. Things moved faster than I anticipated, and I wanted something close to the school." Elizabeth heard the sound of a spoon being stirred. "The farmer certainly appreciates it. He's got someone to look after the animals when he goes on holiday. He and his wife haven't been on holiday for some time, so having me around means they get to have a break now the kids are out of the house."

Elizabeth turned.

"He doesn't have anyone working for him?"

"Not all the time, and I'm right next door. That certainly helps me with working out, lugging the feed around."

David picked up the mugs and walked over to her. He still hadn't put a shirt on, and Elizabeth couldn't look away. Now he was teasing her. It was unfair that he could walk around looking this good, and she wasn't allowed to do anything about it.

"You okay?" David asked as he handed her a mug, their fingers brushing. "You're looking a bit flushed."

"Do you normally walk around half-naked when you've got a guest?"

"What? Oh." David looked down at himself. "Sorry, I forget myself at times. When I'm at home, I don't tend to wear many clothes."

"Oh, really?"

A lot of images went through Elizabeth's mind. Most of them involved David walking around his house naked. Maybe she should suggest that he didn't stop on her account...

"How are you holding up?"

Elizabeth jumped. David had moved over to the kitchen table, putting his steaming mug to one side as he reached for a red t-shirt. Her disappointment flared up as she watched him put it on, the muscles shifting when he lifted his arms. Why did she have to open her big mouth?

"I...I don't really know. It just feels so surreal." Elizabeth leaned against the windowsill, feeling her legs tremble. "This is something you read about in the news, and it feels like a world away. Like when the Suffolk Strangler was on the loose in 2006. I had just started university, but knowing it wasn't that far away from where I spent most of my teen years was unsettling."

"I understand what you're saying." David straightened his t-shirt and adjusted his glasses as one of the legs came off his ear. "It's not until something horrific hits close to home that you realise that you're not invincible. Especially when you feel emotionally invested."

There was a slight change to his voice that Elizabeth noticed. She sipped her coffee, peering at him over the rim of her mug.

"You lost someone, didn't you?"

David stiffened.

"What makes you say that?"

"I can tell. I have worked with you for two years, David. I like to think that I know you well enough."

"You may not know me as well as you think, Elizabeth." Stony-faced, David picked up his mug and took a healthy gulp of coffee. "But you're right. I lost someone. My little sister."

He was trying to keep himself composed, but Elizabeth saw the flash of pain in his eyes. She was an only child; she couldn't begin to imagine how he felt losing a sibling.

"You two were close, weren't you?"

"Yeah. She was a sweetheart. Clever, kind, determined. She always had a smile on her face."

"And what happened?"

"She was murdered. By someone she was supposed to trust." David shook his head and raised his mug to his lips. "I don't like talking about it. It's something I'm not comfortable discussing."

"I'm sorry."

Elizabeth wanted to know more. She wanted to be the one

David confided in, the one he leaned on when he was in need of it. Even now she wished that she could put her arms around him, seeing him hiding his obvious pain.

"Do you think we're going to be next?" she asked.

"It's a possibility." David pulled out a chair at the table and sat down. "But I don't want to speculate. That just makes it dangerous, and it could be farther from the truth than we expect."

"I suppose." Elizabeth wasn't sure how to respond to that. "It's just people I've known since I was a kid are dead, and I wasn't far away from them. That's enough to chill the spine."

David peered at her curiously.

"You said before that you used to be a student at Wolsey, right? Were Isabella and Miles teachers then?"

"Yes. Isabella was not married then. She was relatively new. Miles had been there about ten years, by that point."

"And what did you think of them?"

"Miles was easygoing. Pretty much let us get on with whatever we wanted when he was our teacher. Isabella was still finding her footing, but when she was on the mark she was good. We got on really well."

"I see," David murmured. He was watching her, and the look was making Elizabeth's whole body tingle. Why did it have to be so intense? "So you never saw her assault any of the students? You never witnessed anything that could suggest that she was abusive?"

Elizabeth tensed. She shook her head.

"No. I didn't."

"Because that sort of behaviour doesn't come out of nowhere. It's something that is taught or learned..."

"Isabella never hurt anyone. She did what she had to do in

137

her position."

"And that includes beating a child enough that they have to be sent to the hospital?"

"That's not what I meant."

David grunted.

"Well, I've been having doubts about her for a while. I wouldn't be surprised if someone she beat took matters into their own hands."

Elizabeth was shaking her head before he had finished.

"No, I don't believe it. Isabella was loved by everyone."

"Someone was pissed off enough to kill her."

"Then why kill Miles? He never hurt anyone."

"Maybe he saw something and said nothing. Those who do nothing can also be guilty by association." David sighed and sipped his coffee. "Sorry, Elizabeth. I'm just talking out of my backside right now. I'm trying to make sense of everything, and I'm coming up empty."

Elizabeth managed a small smile.

"It's not exactly something you wanted at the beginning of your time as headteacher, was it?"

"It definitely wasn't in the manual." David put his mug down and took off his glasses, rubbing at his eyes. "It's certainly a situation that is never going to be in control. Not from my perspective, anyway."

"I'm thinking the same thing." Elizabeth took a deep breath. There was a tightness around her chest, and it wasn't easing. "I just hope we can find the maniac before they kill someone else."

David didn't answer. He had put his glasses aside and was massaging his temples. He looked to be in pain. Elizabeth put her mug on the table and moved towards him.

"You okay?"

"I'm fine. It's just a headache." David lowered his hands. "Migraines are a bitch."

"I get that." Taking a bit of courage that had left her for a while, Elizabeth put her hands on his shoulders. "A massage of the head and neck normally works. That's what I've..."

She gasped when David stood up and moved away from him. He moved towards the window, his shoulders tight as he leaned on the windowsill with his bowed. Elizabeth watched him, her courage disappearing as quickly as it had come. What had just happened there? Had she pushed it too far?

"I'm sorry. I'm not really good company right now." David didn't turn around, his voice sounding muffled. "Too much has happened in the last couple of days. And what you're offering couldn't have come at the wrong time."

"What?" Elizabeth faltered. "I wasn't..."

"You were. You've been making things clear since I arrived here." David turned to face him, giving her an apologetic grimace. "Don't get me wrong, I'm flattered. If the circumstances were different, I would have taken you up on your offer a long time ago. But with so much uncertainty in the air, it's probably not appropriate to think about anything sexual."

God, he really did know. Now Elizabeth wanted to find a corner to hide in from embarrassment. She gulped.

"I'm sorry."

"What are you sorry for?"

"I...I'm not..."

David sighed.

"I'm the one who's sorry. I can't be what you want. Not yet, anyway."

"What about after this mess is settled?" Elizabeth asked,

lifting her chin and trying to find her confidence. It seemed to flee whenever David was around, and she hated that. "What then?"

"I'll let you know." David nodded at her mug. "Drink up, and I'll drive you home. I've got things to do, and I'm sure you will want to get back before something happens."

Elizabeth almost wanted to say that she wanted something to happen, but she kept silent. David had, effectively, rejected her, albeit for now. Being bold wasn't going to work; he was a man who didn't change his mind once he had made a decision. That could be sexy, and it had been when they were at work.

But now it was infuriating. Elizabeth didn't like rejection, even if for a short period of time. The feelings when it happened were not pleasant.

Chapter Thirteen

Ellen had no idea how long she had walked for, but her feet were hurting as she arrived back home. Her chest was hurting, and there was an acrid smell in her nostrils. She must have walked by someone who had lit a bonfire; the damn stench was disgusting.

A candle by the bath would be a good idea right now.

As she approached the house, Ellen noticed that Jake's car was outside the house, parked a little haphazardly and almost blocking the road. It looked like he had just skidded the car to a stop before getting out. That was not like him at all.

Had something happened? Had Clara called Jake because she found Ellen had gone? Ellen sighed. She was not looking forward to this.

Taking a deep breath and wishing she could smell something other than that fucking bonfire, Ellen let herself into the house. There was a stillness in the house that settled on her almost immediately, and Ellen felt the agitation building. Something was wrong, she just knew it.

Oh, God, were Jake and Clara okay?

"Jake?" Trying not to panic, Ellen hurried into the kitchen and then the dining room. "Clara?"

Clara's laptop and her work documents were still on the table.

Nothing seemed disturbed, except for a large envelope lying on the open laptop, the screen black. It wasn't like Clara at all to leave that out of place.

"Open it."

Ellen gasped and spun around. Jake and Clara were sitting on the sofa in the living room. Both of them were staring at her with blank expressions. Ellen had never seen either of them like this.

"What...what's going on?"

"Open the envelope, Ellen," Jake repeated. "Look at the contents."

"What's in it?"

Jake didn't answer, and Clara didn't say anything, either. Ellen was getting concerned. It was like they were privy to something that she wasn't, and she didn't like it. That was not fair. But they were not going to tell her.

Trying not to show her frustration, Ellen picked up the envelope and reached inside. There were quite a few papers. No, not papers. They were too thick, and they felt smooth on one side.

Were these photographs?

Not sure she wanted to look at them, Ellen got them out. And dropped them onto the table when she realised what she was looking at. They were of her and Miles. It looked as if someone had been at a distance with a zoom lens, capturing her in an embrace with a man who wasn't her husband.

One was of her and Miles leaving a pub, another was in the car park sharing a kiss. Miles had a hand under her dress as they leaned against his car, Ellen reaching between them and her hand disappearing out of sight. But it was pretty obvious what she was doing.

Ellen's heart sank to her feet. Oh, God, not this. Not now.

"Well?"

Jake's voice had a bite to it. Ellen looked up and saw that he was leaning forward, his gaze ice-cold.

"What do you want me to say? What the hell are these?"

"They're showing that you and Miles Sims have been having an affair."

"No!" Ellen couldn't believe this was happening. She stared at her husband. "What the hell have you been doing? Are you stalking me?"

"They were posted through the door about an hour ago," Clara said quietly. She sounded like she was close to tears. "It had my name on it. As soon as I opened it and saw what was inside, I called Dad. Then I found that you were gone. Where the hell were you?"

"I...I went for a walk."

"And who were you with, Mum?"

Ellen stared. They actually believed it.

"You believe that I've had an affair? Those pictures are doctored! I've never had an affair with Miles."

Jake barked out a harsh laugh.

"Are you kidding me? Proof of your affair was sent to our daughter, and you're saying they're doctored?"

"Of course they are!"

"How did they manage to photoshop you and Miles together? If it is photoshop, it's a fucking amazing job." Jake shot to his feet and strode over, snatching up one of the pictures and holding it up. "That dress you're wearing was what I gave you for your birthday. You said you would wear it for the first time at our anniversary last year. And you're wearing it for Miles!"

"Jake..."

"No, Ellen! I'm not hearing it!" Jake threw the photograph back onto the table. His face was red, and he was breathing heavily. "I can't believe you. I trusted you for so many years, and you kept breaking it. Time and time again, you break it, and I have to put it back together. Not anymore, Ellen. I can't do it any longer."

Ellen couldn't believe what she was hearing. Jake was going off the rails. Her husband hadn't raised his voice like this in years, and she couldn't remember the last time she had seen him this angry. She swallowed, and tried to get her frustration and panic under control. She needed to get this situation back on track and with her in the driving wheel. That's how it was.

She wasn't about to be talked to like this.

"Jake, why don't we sit down and talk about this?"

"No! Don't you dare try and justify or make excuses! You've cheated on me again!" Jake slammed a hand onto the chair, the slap making Ellen jump. "I caught you and Miles together before, remember? Or are you claiming that didn't happen? You certainly like to say that when you're not on your medication. Almost as if it's an excuse for being a sex-mad bitch."

He might as well have slapped her. Ellen suddenly felt cold. How could he have known?

"What are...? I've been taking my medication. You watch me every morning!"

"And I've also witnessed you take it out of your mouth and put it in the bin when you think I'm not looking. God only knows how long you've been doing this, Ellen." Jake folded his arms. "Your condition is not under control, no matter what you say. The doctor said you had to take your medication..."

"I don't need it!" Ellen cried. "There is nothing wrong with me!"

"You have schizoaffective disorder, Mum," Clara pointed out. "That's not something you can handle without medication."

"I do not have schizoaffective disorder!" Ellen pushed past Jake and strode towards her daughter, who stood up quickly and backed away. "The doctor is a quack. I'm perfectly fine!"

"To the point you see things that are not there and fuck anyone that moves if they show interest in you," Jake said sharply.

"No! I had an affair with Miles years ago, yes, but I haven't been with him since."

"That's not what the photographs say."

"They're doctored!" Ellen looked pleadingly at her husband. "Jake, please believe me. I will admit that I haven't taken my medication in a while, but I haven't had an affair with Miles. I wouldn't do that to you."

"You did it to Dad before," Clara's voice was quiet. "What's to say you won't do it again?"

Ellen barked out a sharp laugh.

"Well, it's not going to happen anymore, seeing as Miles is dead."

"But it could happen again. If it hasn't happened already."

"I had an affair once! Your father knows about it!"

Ellen wanted to tear her hair out. Nobody was listening to her, and she was losing control. This couldn't be happening. Not now. She pressed her hands to her chest and took a few deep breaths. There was silence except for her heavy, slow breathing. When Ellen felt like she was more in control and not about to have a panic attack, she turned to Jake.

"Can we talk, Jake? I can explain what's going on, and it's not that."

"There's nothing to explain, Ellen." Jake shook his head. "I forgave you the last time, but I warned you that it was your final warning, and I wasn't going to forgive you again. If you cheated again, I would be leaving."

Ellen stared.

"What? I never heard you say that."

"You said that you understood, and you would work hard to make it up to me."

"I tell you, we never had that conversation."

Jake grunted.

"Of course you would say that. You like to twist things to your own reality. If it doesn't fit your narrative, you're not interested. It wouldn't be the first time."

Ellen gasped.

"I never do that!"

Clara snorted.

"Give over, Mum! You do it all the time! Remember that girl you had all of your friends torment because you believed their parents had taken away some of your power and you wanted to get your own back? The one who died from being hit by a car?"

Ellen went cold. Jane Christian again?

"You don't know anything about that situation, Clara."

"I was in the same class as her brother. Sean saw what you did, and I would find him crying because he saw his sister in pain. Nine years old, and he couldn't do anything about it." Clara's eyes were now filled with tears. "Had they stayed and he had gone into upper prep, would you have hurt him as well? Would you have bullied him until he died?"

"I never laid a finger on that girl!"

"The lawsuit said otherwise, Ellen."

Ellen froze. Jake's voice was like ice, and the words cut right through her.

"What lawsuit?"

Jake groaned.

"Come off it, Ellen. I know it was twenty years ago, but you can't have forgotten how we had to pay the Christian family a settlement. They sued the school, and you were named in the suit."

"I don't remember that."

"Of course you wouldn't. Because you believed you hadn't done anything wrong. We agreed to an amount and I paid for you so we didn't get it dragged out."

"But there was no evidence that we had done anything! Just the words of a dead girl."

Jake's jaw tightened. He stepped towards her, and Ellen found herself backing up. She had never feared her husband like this.

"It may have been just her word, but it was enough to ruin the reputation of the school. You, Isabella, Miles, Kerry, Lisa...all of you thought it was a good idea to bully a twelve-year-old *child* because of something you believed their parents had done to you. You even got your favourite student to put her hands on Jane so you could say you never laid a finger on her. You used that kid like a dog, and she lapped up what she did. All of that was revealed at the time."

"You...you don't..." Ellen licked her lips. It felt like everything was crumbling around her. "You don't believe that I would do that, do you? I've been teaching for thirty years."

"And how many other kids have you tormented?"

"I haven't!"

Jake held up a hand.

"I wasn't sure what to believe at the time, and I gave you the benefit of the doubt back then. I paid because I wanted

147

to protect you. Now with Isabella's court case and the clear evidence, it makes me wonder if what you were accused of was true. You did mentor her, after all. She had to have learned that behaviour from somewhere."

Ellen's chest was tightening to the point she couldn't breathe. She sagged onto the sofa, seeing the disgust in her husband's eyes, and disappointment on her daughter's face.

"This is all false," Ellen managed to say. "I've never bullied a child. I've never put my hands on my students. And I didn't sleep with Miles after that one time."

"You can say that all you want, but it's not going to make anything better." Jake nodded at Clara. "Get your things together, Clara. It's about time we left."

"What?" Ellen's head snapped up. "You're leaving?"

"Of course we are," Clara scoffed as she went towards the dining table and began to pack her things. "You think we would want to be around you after finding out you've made a fool out of Dad?"

"I didn't..."

"Save it, Ellen," Jake snapped. "You're not going to change our minds. Unless you want to tell me where you go without warning and without telling us what you've been up to? You've been doing that a lot recently. Where were you just now?"

Ellen's mouth opened and closed before her brain managed to kick in to help her form words.

"I just went out for a walk. I needed some air, that's all."

"Oh, really? Did you go out for a late-night 'walk' the night Isabella died as well?" Jake sneered. "Because one of the pictures is of you and Miles, and you're wearing what you wore when you went out that night."

"What?"

"Were you and Miles having a 'walk' that night? Is he the only one?"

"Jake!"

Ellen wanted to scream. Jake, her calm and dependable husband, was turning on her. He was believing everything in front of him. She reached towards him.

"Please, it's not what it looks like."

"I don't want to hear it. I'm sure it's going to be a load of bullshit, anyway." Jake turned to their daughter. "Ready to go?"

"Sure am." Clara cast her mother a dark look as she slung her bag over her shoulder. "I can't believe you would be so vocal about people cheating and telling lies, and yet you're the biggest hypocrite I've ever met."

"Clara!" Ellen felt the tears prickling at her eyes, and she tried to blink them back. "Please believe me. I never cheated on your dad. I've never hurt a child. Please..."

The look in her daughter's eyes hurt. A lot. Ellen hadn't thought that she would be in so much pain knowing that her daughter might actually hate her. She didn't think it would happen.

"Let's go, Clara." Jake put a hand on Clara's back and guided her towards the door, shooting Ellen one last look. "We'll give your mother some space. She's got a lot to think about."

"Don't leave me," Ellen whispered.

But she didn't get a response. Father and daughter left, and a moment later, the front door opened and closed. Ellen remained frozen on the sofa as she saw her husband's car move out of sight, pulling away from the house.

It was then that she let the floodgates open.

* * *

Ellen had no idea how long she slept, but when she woke it was dark. She couldn't see anything, even with the moonlight shining in through the window. Fumbling around, she found the lamp and switched it out. God, how was it the middle of summer and it was freezing?

Shivering, Ellen got up and stretched. Her legs were cramped from being curled up for so long, her muscles screaming at her. She stumbled through the house and up the stairs. It took longer than she anticipated, her body not used to moving after being in the same position. Ellen wondered if she should have a bath to try and soothe her, but the thought of sinking below the water and not coming back up again entered her head and wouldn't leave.

Not a good idea, even if it was tempting.

As she changed, Ellen looked down at her legs. She could see the scars criss-crossing her thighs, looking like the cellulite markings she had accumulated from her pregnancies. They were easy enough to pass off as stretch marks to anyone who asked, and nobody looked too closely.

They were easier to hide than ones on her arms, so were the ones on her stomach.

Jake had found out early on in their relationship how Ellen coped when things weren't going her way. He got her to see that it wasn't healthy, and she needed to let it out in a different way. Find a hobby. Ellen took that to heart.

Now she was beginning to regret finding a different way to get rid of the frustration and aggression inside her when something was out of her control.

Jane might still be alive if you had done things differently.

That was not my fault.

Ellen felt anger stirring in her belly as she thought about that girl. The little brat had been dead for decades, and she was still causing trouble. I thought she would be an easy target, but she's brought so much aggravation. And that family of hers. If they hadn't tried to be too big for their boots and swan around like they owned the place, none of this would have happened.

They should have stayed in their lane. It was their fault that their daughter died. She probably wouldn't have made it in life if she didn't have a thick skin. If she couldn't take what she deserved, then what chance did she have?

You still orchestrated horrible things towards her.

I didn't say to go that far.

But you didn't stop it. Because you liked seeing her suffer.

Ellen stared at herself in the mirror. She looked exhausted, and her hair was a mess with dark circles under her eyes, and her skin was really pale. Only a few days ago, she was looking healthy and happy. Who could imagine that things could change so rapidly in such a short space of time?

Someone was screwing with her life. They were trying to drag her through hell. Once Ellen found out who the bastard was doing this, she was going to make sure they regretted bringing all of this out in the open. Nobody screwed with her secrets unless they had some sort of death wish.

Dressing in simple yoga pants and a baggy t-shirt that hit her mid-thigh, Ellen tied her hair back and took a few deep breaths. She still looked tired when she glanced in the mirror, but it wasn't as bad as a few minutes ago.

Maybe a shower later would help. That should clear away some of the numbness.

Ellen headed downstairs, retrieving her laptop from the

living room and opening it up in the kitchen. As she fixed herself a coffee, she opened up her social media. When things were getting tough, looking through social media was one way to cool down. Somehow, the drama that popped up complaining about something or having an internet argument made Ellen feel better. She had a strange satisfaction knowing that it wasn't just her life that was feeling crap.

Although she doubted anyone could match what was happening to her right now.

A buzzing noise reached her ears, and it took a moment for Ellen to remember that it was her phone. Fuck, where had she left it? It sounded really far away.

In the hall. Where she had put it when she slipped out of the house.

Grumbling under her breath, Ellen hurried through the house and snatched the phone up just as it stopped ringing. Maybe it was Jake. Or it could have been Mark; he was going to make his way here to help. He would be on Ellen's side. He listened to his mum.

But it was from a number Ellen didn't recognise. That made her heart sink. Probably one of those stupid cold callers again. Those people seemed to come out of the woodwork when you didn't want them.

That was a nightmare in itself.

As she was about to put the phone down, it started beeping. A text message was coming in. More than likely telling her she had a voicemail, but Ellen opened it anyway. She was surprised to see that it was actually a picture.

Curiosity got the better of it, she tapped the icon. And the screen was filled with a picture of Jane. She was sitting cross-legged on the grass in her uniform, holding onto her violin with a shy smile at the camera. It was an innocent enough smile, but there seemed to be something sinister about it.

Then Ellen noticed the message underneath it.

Are you feeling guilty now?

"Fuck you."

Ellen deleted the message, her phone slipping from her fingers when it started ringing again. Growling, Ellen answered.

"Now look here, you fucking bastard," she snarled. "If you keep contacting me, then I'm going to get the police on you. Do you hear?"

"What the hell, Ellen?"

It took a moment for the words to sink in. Ellen groaned and slumped back onto the bed.

"Sorry, Lisa. I've been having a bad day."

"You and me both. Nora and I are going to head to the coast for the weekend. Given everything going on, the last thing we want to do is stay around while some maniac is wandering about."

"Right." Ellen closed her eyes. Her headache was building again, and there was a throbbing starting behind her eyes. "That sounds like a good idea. I wish I could do that myself."

"What's wrong? Did something happen?"

"It's a long story."

Ellen wanted to tell her friend about Jake and what he found out, but she didn't want to ruin the mood for Lisa. She would be distracted, and Nora wouldn't be too impressed. The woman was too protective of her partner; she could get upset, even at Ellen, if Lisa was in a mood that she didn't like.

How Lisa put up with someone like that, Ellen had no idea.

"Are you sure? You know you can talk to me about things, right?"

"I know. There's just so much going on right now. I think it's going to be a while before I've got my thoughts in order."

"And you'll let me know once that happens?"

"Of course." Ellen hadn't shied away from that yet. Lisa was a really good listener. "You go and enjoy yourself. Are you going to Cromer again?"

"Yes. We'll be back on Monday afternoon. If you need me once I get back, just let me know." Lisa hesitated. "It does feel like I'm running away from things, leaving like this when people are getting murdered, but we spoke to the police and left our details with them, so it's not like we'll get into trouble."

Ellen smiled.

"I don't think anyone could say that you ran away from things, Lisa. You always charged head-first into anything we did."

"Mostly because you told me to. I do as I'm told."

"Which is a good quality." Ellen paused. The picture she had been sent was still fresh in her mind. "Do you think about what happened all those years ago? When we were younger and healthier?"

Lisa was silent for a moment.

"Are you talking about what I think..."

"I am. Do you think about it?"

"Occasionally. I do feel some guilt over what happened. After all, she was just a kid."

"You know the reasons, Lisa," Ellen reminded her.

"I do, and I am not going to excuse anything. But when I saw her body and heard about..." Lisa audibly swallowed. "Let's just say guilt creeps in when I don't want it to."

Ellen wondered if Lisa's conscience was getting to her. Ever since she got together with Nora eighteen years ago, her hardened exterior kept softening. It was close to cracking completely, her hardened friend almost gone. Ellen wondered if she should have a word with Nora about it; she didn't like her friend changing too much.

"Anyway, we're off," Lisa said, her voice dragging Ellen out of her wayward thoughts. "We don't get much signal up on the coast, so it might take a while to get back to you. But you stay safe, okay?"

"I'll try," Ellen murmured.

That's easier said than done when my husband knows what I've been up to.

Hanging up, Ellen slowly made her way upstairs to the empty bedroom. She lay on the bed staring at the ceiling, wondering if there was any point doing anything tonight except watch the TV. She could give the fish and chip shop down the road and get them to deliver for her if she asked very nicely; she didn't feel like going out again, and now couldn't be bothered to cook.

It was surprising how much of her mood hung on having Jake around. Even when she was off her medication, he had kept her on an even keel because he was supportive and understanding. Now that was gone, and she didn't know if it was coming back, Ellen felt like she was floundering around, and it scared her.

Ellen awoke when she heard a loud banging on the door. Shit, hadn't she fallen asleep again? She checked her phone. Only a few minutes had passed. At least she hadn't passed out again.

Feeling sluggish as she sat up, Ellen took a moment for the world to stabilise before she stood up. It felt like she had drunk a bit too much as she made her way onto the landing.

A glass of wine or two would be perfect right about now. Although after finishing off a bottle yesterday, maybe she should slow up a bit. Ellen craved a drink, but she couldn't do it. If Jake came back and she was drunk, that was just going to make things worse.

Still, the urge to get something to drink was present as she walked heavily down the stairs. Whoever was at the door had better have a good reason for bothering her. Ellen was not going to go easy on them.

"Ellen? Ellen, are you there?"

Ellen stopped. What was she doing here? Trying not to fall as she missed the bottom step, Ellen got to the front door and opened it. Leanne was outside, now dressed in jeans and a dark blue t-shirt that hugged her slim frame. Not for the first time, Ellen felt envious looking at the younger woman. How did she manage to look that good? While Ellen's figure was decent and got several looks, it wouldn't be on the same level as Leanne's.

"Ellen?"

Ellen jumped when a hand was waved in front of her face, Leanne looking at her oddly. She shook herself.

"Oh. Sorry, Leanne. I've just woken up."

"You okay?" Leanne looked her up and down. "You look terrible."

"And you're as complimentary as ever." Ellen rubbed at her eyes. "What do you want? If it's about our interaction earlier..."

"No, it's nothing to do with that. I was wondering if Kerry was here."

"What? Kerry?" Ellen wondered if she had missed something. "No, she isn't. Why did you think that?"

"She called me earlier and asked if she could stay with me tonight. Apparently, her husband had to leave for business, and she didn't want to be on her own, so she asked if she could spend the night at my place."

Now Ellen felt even more confused. Leanne and Kerry didn't

really get along, their personalities like oil and water. To have Kerry asking someone she didn't like if they could spend the night together because she was scared of being alone didn't sound right.

"Why did she ask you?"

"I have genuinely no idea, but I wasn't about to say no." Leanne hesitated. "After all, I would have been alone, and I've been jumping at shadows."

"Oh?" Ellen couldn't help but add a slight quip. "I thought you would have spent it with David. You two are pretty close."

Leanne frowned.

"I'm not interested in David like that. Besides, I hate the stench coming from the farm, so I'd rather spend the night alone than with him."

Ellen couldn't argue with that. If the wind blew in a certain direction, they could smell the farm from the school. It wasn't pleasant. How David put up with it, Ellen had no idea. He probably had no sense of smell.

"Well, Kerry's not here. Maybe she changed her mind and decided to stay? She does have a tendency to dither on things."

"I suppose so." Leanne looked uncertain. "But I've been calling her all afternoon, and she's not picking up. Normally, I wouldn't give it much thought, but with what happened to Isabella and Miles, I'm getting nervous."

"I see your point." Ellen noticed a dark shape parked to her right. "Do you mind if you drive? I can give you directions. She's only in the next village, but the houses are not marked very clearly."

"Sure. Sorry to bother you about this, Ellen."

"It's fine. I need something to distract myself right now." Grabbing her keys and phone, Ellen shoved her feet into her trainers and stepped out into warm darkness. "Although, given the time, she's probably asleep by now. She's more than likely going to be annoyed at us for waking her up."

"As long as she's okay, I'll cope with that."

Ellen silently agreed. Kerry did have a tendency to go back and forth on decisions when she was left in charge, but she never missed a phone call. Hopefully, all that had happened was that she had fallen asleep.

Hopefully.

Chapter Fourteen

It only took five minutes to get to Kerry's house, although the winding black road made it feel like the journey went even longer. Ellen didn't think she would ever get used to driving from light to dark so abruptly, even after living there for as long as she had. It was something that took a moment to get used to behind the wheel.

Being in the passenger seat somehow felt worse. What the hell were they doing going to find someone at this time of night? Maybe Kerry really had fallen asleep. Perhaps she forgot that she called Leanne. All of them were stressed, and Kerry was known for taking naps when things got too much for her.

That had to be it.

Leanne followed Ellen's directions and pulled into the driveway. The lights were off, but the curtains were open. Kerry's car was also in the driveway, parking in its usual spot in front of the garage. At least she was home.

Squinting in the dark, Ellen got out and went up to the front door. She knocked and waited. Nothing. Then she tried the bell. Still nothing. There was no movement inside at all.

"Either she's passed out or nobody's home," she said, turning to Leanne as the younger woman joined her.

"Or the third option," Leanne commented, looking up at the

house. "And I don't want to contemplate what it might be."

Ellen shook her head.

"Honestly, you've been watching too many horror movies."

"What can I say? It's my favourite."

Ellen grunted. Then she pointed towards the side of the house.

"Why don't you go around the back and see if you can look in through the window? The gate is just on a latch, so there shouldn't be a problem."

"What are you going to do?"

"I'll keep trying the front door. Hopefully, we can make enough noise that we can wake her up."

Then Ellen was going to scold Kerry for freaking them out. Not being able to contact her was making Ellen uncomfortable. What if something had happened to her?

No, that couldn't be the case. Kerry was a fighter. If something happened, she would be making sure the one attacking her came off worse. Ellen was sure that this was just a misunderstanding.

Even as she thought that, she couldn't shake the churning in her stomach that was starting to knot into a tight ball.

Ellen turned as light appeared and illuminated her against the door. She turned and saw a car coming into the driveway. Momentarily blinded, she shield her eyes until the light moved and she could see properly. A smart black BMW parked next to Kerry's car, and the driver got out.

"Ellen? What are you doing here?"

With the black dots in front of her eyes, it took a second for Ellen to figure out who was in front of her. She blinked rapidly, trying to get rid of the dots.

"Sam?"

"Who else?" Sam approached her. "What's going on?"

"I'm not sure." Ellen gestured towards the house. "Kerry called Leanne earlier, asking to stay with her tonight. But she never turned up, and I'm not getting an answer."

Sam looked up at the house, the darkness hiding the expression on his face. Somehow, that made him look more sinister, and Ellen tried not to shiver. She wished that she had brought a jacket as well.

"I've been trying to get hold of Kerry as well," Sam said quietly. "I thought she was with you: she often ignores my calls whenever you two are together."

Ellen ignored that jab in her direction.

"I thought you were on business, although I thought it was odd with it being a bank holiday."

"I thought so, too, but someone had to go. Not everyone stopped working on a bank holiday." Sam sighed. "But when I got there, I found that the guy who had supposedly gone off sick and couldn't do it was actually there. He was as confused as I was that I had turned up as well. So we went over the brief together, had drinks and then I decided to drive back. Given how uncomfortable Kerry was after what happened at the school, I didn't want to leave her longer than I absolutely had to."

Somehow, that explanation fell flat on Ellen. Sam was never that good of a liar, but lawyers were slippery characters. Although despite his faults, he did love Kerry. A little overprotective at times, but Kerry said that was how Sam was.

He would never hurt her. Would he?

"I couldn't see anyone back...oh." Ellen looked past Sam to see the shape of Leanne appear and stop when she saw them. "Sam? I thought you were away."

"Well, I'm back now. You said you couldn't see anyone?"

Leanne's head moved in the dark.

"No. The curtains are open, and there's no one in sight."

"And her car's here." Ellen nodded over at the vehicle. "She has to be inside. Maybe she's asleep."

"She would always close the curtains, though," Sam pointed out. "And when she's nervous, she keeps all the lights on. Something about not wanting to jump at shadows."

"Maybe she fell asleep before the need to close the curtains?" Leanne suggested.

Sam didn't answer. He just fished into his pocket and withdrew his keys, jangling them about his fingers.

"I hope that's the case," he muttered. "But we're not going to find out standing on the doorstep."

"I couldn't agree more," Ellen said.

Sam shot her a look Ellen couldn't see properly, but the chill in the air was enough. He thought that she was a meddler who liked to be in charge all the time, that she didn't like anyone taking that authority.

There was no need to think about it. Ellen did like to be in charge.

Sam let them into the house, switching on the lights. The hall and upstairs landing became illuminated. As Ellen shut the door, Leanne switched on the lights in the living room.

"There's no one in here. I'll double-check the kitchen."

"Try our office," Sam said. "Sometimes, she holes herself up in there and she forgets the time. I'll look upstairs."

Not wanting to be left hanging around, Ellen followed him up the stairs. As she climbed, she became aware of a strange smell hanging in the air. It reminded her of when Jake's brother burned the meat on the barbecue the previous summer. There was also a pungent odour that made her stomach retch.

"Oh, God." She clamped a hand over her mouth and nose. "What is that smell?"

"I think I know." Sam paused at the top of the stairs. "Ellen, I think you'd better go back downstairs."

"Why?"

Sam swallowed. His face had gone white, and he looked like he was going to collapse as he stared at the partially open door before him.

"Because I don't think you should come any further." He held up a hand as Ellen started to speak. "Don't argue with me, Ellen. Just...go and call the police. And maybe an ambulance."

"What? An ambulance?"

Ellen hurried up the stairs and barged past Sam. He tried to grab her, but Ellen yanked her arm away and pushed Sam aside, causing him to stumble into the wall. Ignoring his groan, she pushed open the door and entered the room.

Only to be hit with the stench, a mixture of burned flesh and vomit. It made her stomach lurch, and Ellen buckled over with a moan. For a moment, all she was experiencing was how the smell hit her like a physical wall.

Through her watering eyes, Ellen saw the mess on the bed. It was a body, or it looked like a body. With the huge welts that were blisters and the melted skin, it felt like she had walked into a Clive Barker novel. The body was tied to the brass bars of the bed ends, looking like a sacrifice. Blood and vomit were on the pillow, encrusted around the lips and eyes closed. But the burns were evident.

Even with the disfigured face, Ellen didn't need to know who it was.

"Oh, fuck!"

Ellen screamed as someone grabbed onto her, and she lashed out.

"Let me go! Get your hands off me!"

"We have to leave, Ellen!" Sam pulled her towards the door. "This is a crime scene now!"

"What about Kerry?"

"There's nothing we can do for her." Sam's voice broke, not looking at her or the body as they left the room. "She's already gone."

"How the fuck do you know? We could try..."

"Just shut up!"

Sam shoved her, causing Ellen to stumble back and hit the wall. Her legs gave way, and she ended up sitting hard on the floor. Stunned from what just happened, Ellen watched as the man collapsed onto his knees, his expression crumbling.

"Just...shut...the fuck...up...you stupid...bitch."

Then he buried his face in his hands and started to wail.

* * *

Ellen couldn't see. It was dark, and she was stumbling everywhere. Where the hell was the light? Was there any light at all?

Then she saw her house. It was too far away, but it was there. Ellen started to run. Her lungs were burning, and she was sobbing, but she finally got there. She lunged at the front door and stumbled into the house.

It was silent, but there was a definite hum in the air. Ellen looked around, trying to figure out what was different. She was home, but it didn't feel like home. Everything felt distorted. Where was Jake? She needed him.

That was when she heard laughter. It was the type that left her cold. And it was coming from inside the house.

Ellen went into the living room, only to freeze in the doorway when she saw the people sitting before her. Isabella was the closest to her, soaking wet with her hair almost obscuring her face. And her stare was ice-cold. Beside her was Miles, sliced up and the welts swelling on his body. His mouth was closed, still in that twisted state Ellen had last seen it. And Kerry was on the other sofa, covered in burns with her skin melting and her eyes closed. She was laughing maniacally, rocking back and forth. The sound was chilling.

"Are you feeling guilty now?"

Ellen turned. And Jane Christian was standing there, wearing the clothes she had on when she died. Her face was white, black shadows around her eyes and blood around her mouth.

"Your friends are dead because of you," Jane hissed. "Are you feeling guilty now?"

Ellen screamed. She lashed out, but her hand went through Jane's face. The girl didn't even flinch, looking at her with such contempt that it was practically dripping from her. Ellen collapsed to her knees in the doorway, her fingers digging into her scalp as she screamed and screamed.

"Ellen! Ellen, wake up!"

Ellen felt hands on her, and she bucked wildly. She hit something, and then clarity began to come back to her. It was a nightmare. She had been dreaming.

She opened her eyes, feeling a firm grip around her wrists. And found David leaning over her. He looked a little odd, different somehow. God, was she seeing things in reality as well?

"David? What...what are you...?"

165

"What am I doing here?" David let go of her and bent over, picking something off the floor. "Leanne called me. You were refusing to go to the hospital and wanted to go home. She was concerned about leaving you alone, so I came to help her look after you."

Ellen watched as he put his glasses back on. She must have knocked them off his face. She grimaced.

"I'm sorry. I didn't mean to hit you."

"Don't worry about it. I've been hit harder." David gave her a gentle smile and sat on the edge of the bed. "I was going to ask how you're feeling, but I think I know the answer."

It was then that the previous night came flooding back. Ellen and Sam had been in hysterics when Leanne found them. She had been the one to call the police, the one who organised everything. For the first time in her life, Ellen was glad that someone else was doing the work and not her; she could still see Kerry's mangled body, and it made her feel worse.

She had been offered an ambulance to get to the hospital, but Ellen had refused. She just wanted to go home and be with her husband. Someone had to get hold of Jake. He had to be there for her.

Everything became a bit of a blur after that. The paramedics had given her a sedative, and it must have made her really sleepy. Her body certainly felt sluggish.

"I...I could see them, David." Ellen shifted upright, adjusting the pillows behind her. "Isabella, Miles, Kerry...they were here. Dead, but very much alive. And they...they wouldn't stop looking at me."

"You were dreaming about them?"

"I don't know about dream. It was more like a nightmare."

Ellen wanted to tell David about Jane, and what she said, but

166

she kept it back. This wasn't something she could confess to him. If David knew the truth, he would report it; the man was too honourable. And Ellen couldn't have her work reputation tarnished because she confessed her sins to the wrong person.

Your reputation is going to be tarnished due to the divorce. People are going to know why in a place like this. News travels fast.

There was a gentle knock at the door, and it opened. Ellen sat up, expecting Jake's head to poke around the door. Her heart sank when she saw Leanne, who was carrying a steaming mug. The younger woman looked tired, but she managed a smile as she approached the bed.

"Hey. I thought you might like a cup of tea. I put in some extra sugar as well."

"Thanks." Ellen attempted a smile in return as she gingerly took the mug. "You've been here all night?"

"We both have. I slept in one of the bedrooms, and David camped out on the sofa downstairs." Leanne glanced at David. "Neither of us were comfortable leaving you alone, especially after what you saw."

Ellen gulped.

"Did...did you see...?"

"No, I didn't go in. The smell and your reaction was enough for me to keep away." Leanne shuddered. "God, I've never seen you and Sam collapse like that. Sam looked broken."

"Where is he now?"

"He actually agreed to go to the hospital. He gave me his sister's number, and she's driving up from Chelmsford to join him at the hospital." Leanne frowned at David and gestured at his face. "You've got a red mark on your face. What happened?"

"Oh, nothing." David gave Ellen a slight smile. "Mrs Lawson reminded me that she still possessed a fierce right hook, even when she's asleep."

Ellen winced.

"Sorry."

"Like I said, I've had worse."

For some reason, Ellen didn't doubt it. She took a sip of the tea. It was hot, and very sweet. It was quite nice, actually. Leanne had a knack of making everyone's tea just how they liked it in the staffroom. She hadn't lost her touch, even in this situation.

"What...what happened to Kerry?"

David and Leanne exchanged looks.

"Do you really want to know?" David asked.

"I need to." Ellen took a deep breath. "Just tell me. What the hell happened to her? And when?"

"Hydrochloric acid." David absently adjusted his glasses. "She had it spilled all over her. Then she was forced to drink it. Her insides had to be burning as much as her outside."

Hydrochloric acid. Ellen had seen that episode of *Poirot* when someone drank acid when they thought it was a glass of water. Even though that had been acting, knowing that it could kill when ingested had left Ellen nervous to pick up her own glass afterwards. And Kerry had that forced that down her throat?

Poor Kerry.

"I'm beginning to panic," Leanne said, wrapping her arms around her middle as she paced away. "That's three people in three days. Who's it going to be today? One of us?"

"Leanne..." David began, but Leanne kept going.

"No, David. Three people from the school are dead now. There are a lot of us, but what if they don't catch whoever is doing this in time and we all get whittled down?"

"Leanne." David held up a hand, his tone gentle but firm.

"Calm down. Nobody else is going to get killed. They're going to catch whoever did this."

"Will they?" Ellen whispered. "Because these murders are getting more and more vicious. And they seem to be well-planned. I'm half-expecting someone to get decapitated."

Leanne shuddered and turned away. David grimaced.

"Maybe we shouldn't think about that. You're making my neck itch with that image."

Ellen's whole body was itching. She didn't care what he was thinking. She sipped her tea.

"Was there a picture of Jane Christian near the body? I didn't have time to see it."

"There was." Leanne sat on the stool by the dresser. "It was pinned to the wall above the bed."

"And the police have found nothing? No fingerprints? No other DNA that can be used?"

"With everyone going in and out of the school, there are going to be thousands of prints." David shook his head. "God knows how long it will take before they find something they can use. Unless someone walks into the police station and says outright that they committed the murders, there isn't anything."

Ellen stared.

"Are they saying they have no idea who could have done this? What about suspects? Are you serious that they have no one?"

"All of us have alibis for the time of the murders, and the Christian family were checked into. They don't live anywhere near here anymore, and they are all accounted for." Leanne glanced at David. "Should we tell her?"

David tensed. Ellen noticed that he was trying not to look at her, finding the pattern on her duvet more interesting. She put her mug on the bedside table.

"What is it? David?"

David didn't respond immediately, looking like he was choosing his words carefully. Ellen sat forward and grabbed his arm.

"David, don't stall for my sake. Tell me what you know."

"It's not about the murders. Not really, anyway." David finally looked up at her. "When the police were talking to Mrs Christian, she talked about Charlie Savedra."

Ellen frowned. She hadn't heard that name in years.

"Charlie? You mean the headteacher from back then?"

"Yes. She was ranting about how he was so weak that he allowed extreme bullying to happen, and that if he had put his foot down Jane would still be alive." David's voice had a bit of a bite to it, and he slowly shifted away from Ellen. "I guess they must have decided to look into him as a suspect or something, from what the inspector told me."

"Inspector Franks?"

David nodded.

"He was there last night. He asked us about Charlie, but he was obviously before my time, so I had no idea about him."

"But I did," Leanne said quietly. "I remember that he was so softly-spoken that I was surprised that he was the headteacher."

Ellen couldn't argue with that. But from the body language between the two people before her, something else was going on.

"Something happened to him? Is he the killer?"

"No, he's not." David sighed and took off his glasses, rubbing his eyes. "He's dead as well."

"What?" Ellen's mouth fell open. "When? How?"

"Just before Christmas two years ago. He had been walking

on Kinder Scout, and he fell and broke his neck." David put his glasses back on. He looked exhausted. "It was deemed an accident, but his wife thought it might have been suicide. She was in the process of separating from him because she found out that her husband had been having an affair. Apparently, their family splitting apart and his sons not talking to him just crushed Charlie. He said that he lived for his kids, and they were refusing to see him."

Ellen felt like she was slipping back into shock. She hadn't spoken to Charlie for a long time, mostly because his contract as the headteacher hadn't been renewed for another year after what happened with Jane, and he had needed to find employment elsewhere. He hadn't fought it at all, and looked almost relieved to get away. Ellen had called him a coward, saying that he was running away from what he had done.

Charlie simply said he was happy to be called a coward because he was one for not standing up to those who thought it was okay to bully a child.

He never did understand.

"Is there a chance that he was murdered as well?" she asked. "It might have been two years ago, but I can't see it being just a coincidence."

"Let's just leave that to the police," David said quietly. "It's best that we do that instead of speculating what could have happened, otherwise we're going to get suspicious of everyone and things might get worse."

"Worse than they already are?" Leanne snorted. She stood up. "I can't do this anymore. This is too much. I didn't come here to see my colleagues get picked off one by one. This isn't an environment for my son."

"Leanne..." David began, but she cut him off.

"No, David! I can't do it. I need to get out of here before I end up a victim myself." Leanne was beginning to hyperventilate. "After all, I was at the school when Jane died. What if the killer thinks I'm to blame as well for not saying anything? What if they kill me as well?"

David stood up and approached her.

"You're not going to end up dead as well," he said gently. "We're all going to be fine."

He touched her shoulders, but Leanne shook him off.

"I can't. I've got a son to think about. Even if they find whoever is doing this before school starts back up again, it's too much." She looked him in the eye. "I quit. I'm out of here. I won't be back for the start of term. Don't try and stop me."

"Leanne..."

But Leanne was already storming out of the room. David looked helpless. Ellen sighed.

"Let her go, David. She'll calm down."

"That's a strange comment to come from the woman who was in a panic in her sleep not too long ago."

"Trust me, I want to panic as well. But it's not doing me any good right now." Ellen drew her knees up to her chest and wrapped her arms around them over the duvet. "I'd love to run away as well, but I can't. I have a feeling this is going to follow me no matter where I go."

David frowned.

"What are you talking about? You think you're going to become the next target?"

"Possibly."

It's highly likely. And I'm scared.

David approached the bed and sat down again, resting a hand on her arm.

"That's not going to happen. Whoever this sick maniac is will be caught, and you'll be safe. It will take time, but we'll get back to normal."

"I suppose," Ellen murmured.

"Look, the police have said we can go back into the school now, and we've got a lot to do before the kids start coming in. We can use that as a distraction and focus on something else. Much as I want to just cut everything off and put it to one side after all this has happened, I know that we have to keep going." David paused. "I like to think I'm good at compartmentalising, but I've never had to deal with anything like this before. You're tougher than I am. Even after all you've been through, you're still so strong. I need that with me right now."

Ellen couldn't help but feel pleased hearing that. Someone needed her. And she could see the truth in David's words. They were needed, and focusing on something else was what they needed. It was the only way they were going to get through this.

And the only way she was going to cope with Jake leaving her. Ellen was sure she would get him back, and they could talk it out, but it was going to take a lot of work.

She managed a smile and put her hand over David's.

"I'll be there. Try getting rid of me."

Chapter Fifteen

When Elizabeth woke up the next morning and saw the text from David that Kerry was dead, she couldn't be more shocked. What the hell was going on? Three murders in three days? Was there going to be a forth?

Oh, God, was she going to be next? Elizabeth had been thinking about it since Miles' body had been found and those pictures of Jane kept popping up out of nowhere. After all, she had been there when Jane was hurt. But she hadn't done anything about the mistreatment. Quite the opposite, actually.

Did someone know she didn't do the right thing and put her on the same list as the other teachers? Someone was picking them all off one by one, and Elizabeth had no idea what the order was.

That scared her. She didn't know what was going on, and she didn't like it. If only she knew what was coming. It would help her feel more in control.

God, the whole situation made her want to scream.

David had asked if she could go over to Ellen's house and stay with her for a while. Jake had left the house, and so Ellen would be on her own. In her current state, David was concerned about her. Of course, because he said it, Elizabeth was texting back yes before she had finished reading the message. Anything to

174

help David out.

She had just finished getting dressed and was dragging a brush through her hair - why were there always knots when she was in a rush - when she could hear her phone ringing. Damn, why now? It had better not be her mother freaking out over the murders yet again and asking Elizabeth to come to London until whoever it was had been caught. It had taken most of yesterday to calm her down, which might have explained why Elizabeth was too drained to do anything the previous evening.

Finding her phone under her pyjamas on the bed, Elizabeth saw Lisa's name flashing up. She schooled her voice into something that didn't sound down and flat before she answered. It wasn't her place to tell her about Kerry just yet, and she didn't want the woman to have her weekend away ruined.

"Hey, Lisa, how is...?"

"Is it true?" Lisa sounded harried. "Is it true that Kerry's dead?"

"What?"

"Tell me!"

Elizabeth flinched at the shriek. It felt like she had been drinking, and the hangover was making her head hurt. It was too early for this.

"Yes, it's true. Kerry's been killed."

"Oh, fuck!" There was the sound of flesh hitting something hard, which made Elizabeth jump. "You have to be fucking kidding me!"

"How did you find out about that?"

"Leanne texted me about it. I saw it when I woke up." Lisa was breathing heavily now, sounding like she was close to hysterics. "God, this is a nightmare. I can't believe this is happening."

Then Elizabeth heard something. Lisa's background made it feel like she was taking the call in a tunnel. There was a loud roaring noise.

"Lisa, where are you?" She stuck a finger in her ear, but blocking out noise had no effect at all. "You sound like you're on the beach."

"No, I'm in the car. We're on our way back."

"What? But I thought you weren't coming back until Monday."

Lisa snorted.

"As if I can stay away after what's happened. Kerry's dead and Ellen needs me. I've got to get back. Oh, be quiet, Nora!"

Elizabeth could hear Lisa's partner saying something that was muffled by the roaring. She could imagine that Nora was not happy about this at all. Whenever something happened with Ellen, Lisa dropped everything for her best friend. Nora ended up being a hanger-on in her own relationship.

She wasn't going to try and dissect that; nothing to do with her.

"It might be best if you stay in Cromer, Lisa." Elizabeth sat on the bed. "Ellen's being looked after, and if people are being killed, you're out of the danger zone."

"Ellen's being looked after? By whom?" Lisa scoffed. "Certainly not by her husband. He's left her, hasn't he?"

"What? When did that happen?"

"Leanne told me. She had to call Jake, and he just said 'not his business' and hung up. I can't believe he would abandon Ellen when she's going through this."

"David is with her right now. I'm going over there as well. She won't be alone."

Lisa sniggered.

"Of course you would. You would do anything David asks."

"What's that supposed to mean?"

"Come on, Elizabeth, we've all noticed how you are around him. True, he's a good-looking guy, but he's never going to be with someone like you. You're below him."

Elizabeth bristled. How could Lisa talk to her like that?

"That's not true!" she protested.

"Be realistic, honey. David probably has a girlfriend some-where. He never talks about his private life like that. With your luck, you'll end up getting between a happy couple."

"David is single, and whether we start something or not is none of your business."

Lisa grunted.

"Maybe not. Just don't come crying to us when he tells you it's never going to happen."

But that was the thing. Elizabeth knew something was going to happen. David had pretty much said it to her. This current mess was in the way, and he was right that it wasn't an appropriate time. But once it was done...

Elizabeth was going to make sure David knew she was not going anywhere. Even if she had to take all of her clothes and offer herself to him. After what was going on, she didn't care about the professional relationship. She was going to have him.

"Anyway, we're almost back," Lisa went on briskly. "Once we get home, I'm coming straight over. I'm not about to leave Ellen to deal with this alone."

"But David and I..."

"You two don't know Ellen like I do. I can look after her."

With a couple of bottles of wine, more than likely.

"Anyway, just let David know I'm almost home. Then he can leave it all to me."

"Lisa..."

Then Lisa hung up, and Elizabeth was listening to intense silence. Groaning, she lowered the phone and slumped over, pressing the corner of her phone into the centre of her forehead. This whole thing was going to be the death of them in one way or another.

If Lisa wanted to implode her relationship with Nora, then that was up to her. Her long-time crush on Ellen was never going to be fulfilled, even now. Nora wasn't going to stand for it any longer.

Before she knew what she was doing, Elizabeth was calling David. If Lisa came barging in, she was just going to disrupt everything. Well-meaning she could be, she had as much subtlety as a battering ram.

David picked up on the third ring.

"Elizabeth? You okay?"

"I'm fine. I'll be on my way out shortly." Elizabeth sighed, wishing she could lean on him right now. "Lisa just called. She's almost back here."

"I thought she was on holiday."

"Did you tell Leanne to let her know about Kerry?"

"I asked her to help me text everyone about it and that everyone needed to stay home for now until everyone had been spoken to." David paused. "I'm guessing Lisa immediately made her way back?"

"Yes. And she's going to come straight over. She's going to agitate Ellen, I'm sure of it."

"They're close. Of course she would want to be here."

Elizabeth snorted.

"You're rather oblivious, David. Lisa has had a crush on Ellen the whole time they've known each other."

"Wait, what? Really?"

Elizabeth couldn't help but smile.

"You really didn't notice?"

"I'm not looking at people in the staffroom and wondering which ones are fucking each other. That's not my business."

"Well, Ellen's straight so she would never do that with Lisa."

But she knew. Elizabeth had guessed pretty quickly when she saw the two that Ellen knew exactly about Lisa's crush. It was how she was able to get Lisa to do whatever she wanted. Including potential crimes. Elizabeth had witnessed it first-hand. Lisa Shaw was the one who fell in line first, even before Miles.

And Ellen toyed with them. She knew how to get what she wanted.

"Elizabeth?"

"Hmm? Oh, sorry." Elizabeth stood up and headed towards the door. "I'm just getting my shoes on and I'll be right over."

"Thanks." David's voice softened. "I'm glad you're around. You're a godsend."

Elizabeth felt her face getting warm. If only she was in front of him now; she would love to finally put her arms around him. To lean into that body and feel his embrace as she snuggled against his chest.

Damn, this crush was bad.

"I try and do my best," she said lightly.

"I know you do. And I'm glad about it. Sometimes, we all need someone to lean on."

"I'm happy for you to lean on me, David."

There was a moment of silence. Then David cleared his throat.

"Right. I...I'm going to check on Ellen again. She's started

179

crying again, and I'm trying to figure out what I can say that won't have her snapping my head off."

"Okay. I'll be there soon."

"Thanks."

Then he hung up. Elizabeth sighed, shoving her phone into her pocket. What was it with simply hanging up nowadays? Did nobody say goodbye anymore?

There was an envelope on the mat. That hadn't been there when she had come down for breakfast earlier. The postman must have come by while she was having a shower.

Although it was strange; she hadn't heard the postman as normal. He was not a quiet person, and he would whistle out of tune as he came up the path. Maybe it was a replacement? Elizabeth would be happy to have a different person delivering her post if it meant things could be quiet.

Picking up the letter, Elizabeth retrieved her trainers and sat on the stairs, turning the envelope over. The address was printed on a sticker, but there was no return mark other than the stamp. And it felt like there was a lot of paper inside.

She should be getting herself out the door and leaving to meet David. But instead she opened the letter. If it was junk mail, Elizabeth wasn't going to be too happy about it.

The papers were folded, and it looked pretty thick. There was a yellow sticky note attached to it, and Elizabeth frowned when she saw the words.

This is you, isn't it? LMP.

LMP? Who the hell was that? Why would they send something to her?

Elizabeth unfolded the papers and read the first few lines. And her stomach dropped.

What the hell? How did they manage to get hold of this? She

thought her record was sealed due to being a juvenile. Yet she had what had been in her file in her hands.

She felt like her heart was having palpitations as she looked over everything. It included a statement from the girls she hurt, detailing everything she had done. Elizabeth's stomach felt like it was going to bring up her breakfast as she read them. She didn't want to, but she couldn't look away. Her trainwreck of a childhood was right in front of her.

On the last page was a scrawled note, barely legible but she could just about read it.

No wonder Queen Bitch chose you. You were perfect.

Her throat closing, Elizabeth threw the papers away. They scattered across the hall, fluttering down to the floor. The page with the note landed face-up near her feet, the words seeming to taunt her.

No, this shouldn't have happened. Nobody knew what she had done before she went to Wolsey Prep. It was supposed to stay that way. The only person who knew was Ellen, and that had only been a few years ago when Elizabeth got too drunk and ended up confessing what she did before she arrived at the school. And she hadn't judged her for it, saying that they all made mistakes, and Elizabeth had more than made up for it.

Had she known the whole time? If that was the case, why would she post these now? But it wasn't her handwriting; Elizabeth had seen it so many times over the years, and she knew it wasn't Ellen.

Although she could be trying to disguise her writing...

No. Elizabeth would not accept it. Ellen had not done this to her. She would have brought it up years ago, not post it anonymously. And Elizabeth had no idea who LMP was.

Whoever they were, they had certainly scared her. They knew

about her past and how she got expelled. Wolsey Prep had meant to be her fresh start, and that's what she did. Have a fresh start.

The past should stay in the past.

* * *

Lisa didn't need to guess that Nora was furious with her. As soon as she woke up and saw the text from Leanne, Lisa knew she had to get back. Ellen was going to need her. How had she managed to be so unlucky to find all three bodies? Someone in hell had to be toying with her.

There had to be some special kind of sadist who allowed that to happen.

This was going to take a lot of smoothing over, though. Nora was shocked that someone else had died, but she was more upset that she had to drive Lisa back. Lisa could have gone on her own, but Nora refused to be left without transport, and she knew Lisa would forget to come back and get her. They either went together or not at all.

Lisa wasn't about to carry on her weekend away. How could she relax now she knew what had happened? There was no question about it: she had to go back.

Nora would understand once she calmed down. She always did.

It felt like forever before they got back, Nora pulling into the driveway so fast that Lisa thought they were going to go through the wall and into the front room. Nora yanked on the handbrake and started getting out.

"Get your things inside," she said sharply. "You don't want to forget anything, do you?"

Lisa sighed.

"Look, Nora..."

"Save it, Lisa. I don't want to hear it." Nora got out. "I don't want to hear you justify why you have to run to Ellen Lawson's side like a fucking lapdog."

"Hey!" Lisa scrambled out. "What's with the attitude? My friend has just been murdered! A third friend, at that! How can you be so insensitive?"

"It's not that I'm upset about. I understand that it's shocking for that to happen in such a short space of time." Nora opened the boot, not looking at her partner as she got the bags out. "It's you immediately wanting to get back for Ellen that I'm pissed off about. As soon as you hear that Ellen is in distress or she tells you to do something, you do it immediately."

Lisa got out. She knew this was a touchy subject with Nora, and Lisa was aware that she had been stupid with it over the years. She did put Ellen before the woman she had been with for years, but she couldn't help it.

She loved Ellen. They had stuck together over the years. And she wanted her to be safe. Who wouldn't drop everything for someone they loved?

"You make it sound like I'm obsessed with her or something," Lisa grumbled.

Nora's head snapped up. Her eyes flashed.

"Of course you're obsessed with her! You've been like this since I met you."

"What?"

"Don't play coy. I saw it as soon as I saw the two of you together. You're obsessed with that bitch, and she laps up the attention. I doubt she sees you as a friend. More like a faithful lapdog because you do as she wants no matter the situation."

Dropping the bags onto the drive, Nora slammed the door shut and glared at Lisa. "I've been with you for almost twenty years, and I've put up with it, for the most part, because I love you and you've shown that you love me, too. But I'll always be second to Ellen. I'll never come first when she's around."

Lisa felt like she had been slapped. Her mouth fell open.

"But..."

"Save it, Lisa. I don't want to hear it. The one time when I was your undivided attention, and she still gets in the fucking way."

"She didn't plan to find Kerry's body!"

Nora grunted, turning away to pick up some of the bags.

"I wouldn't be surprised if it came out that she was the one who murdered the others."

"*WHAT?*"

"You heard me. She's such an egomaniac that she would do this to get attention. And if she is as bad as Isabella was, she would want to make sure that Isabella didn't throw her under the bus. She was her mentor, after all."

Lisa couldn't believe what she was hearing. What she actually suggesting...? No, that couldn't be right.

"Ellen wouldn't murder Isabella. Nor would she murder Miles. And what about Kerry? It doesn't make sense."

"Makes sense to me if Isabella was going to finally tell someone about who started all of the abuse at Wolsey Prep. And Miles and Kerry are weaker than you are; they would crumble once they were pushed, although Miles would try to protect Ellen anyway. The stupid fool didn't think with the right head when it came to the queen of the school." Nora turned to her. "The more I think about it the more it makes sense. And she's going to have a fall guy should she get caught. That would be

184

you."

Lisa snorted.

"Don't be ridiculous. That would never happen."

She saw an icy sheen pass across Nora's face, her expression turning to stone.

"Your reaction tells me that I hit the mark a little closer than I anticipated," she said quietly.

"What are you talking about? We've never hurt any kids."

"What about that girl who was hit by a car? It was you who hit her, wasn't it?"

Lisa went cold. How did she...?

"No! That wasn't me! Jane just ran out in front of a car, that's all!"

"Because she was being chased by one of the many kids who bullied her. She walked from one hell into another, and as a result she didn't get to live as she could have because of you and your little gang who didn't get past the mental age of someone in puberty."

"I never hit her with my car!"

"Are you sure about that? Because the rumours at the time said otherwise. I ignored them because I got to know the real you and thought you wouldn't be so sick as to hit a kid and run away. But with things in recent days, I'm beginning to wonder." Nora blinked hard, and Lisa realised that she was close to tears. "I put my trust in you, and now I realise that I've wasted my time. Eighteen years down the drain because I trusted the wrong person."

Down the drain? What did she mean by that?

"Nora? What...are you saying?"

"I don't know. It could be because I'm still angry over that we had yet another holiday cut short because you had to come back for something Ellen wanted..."

"That's never happened!"

"This is the sixth consecutive holiday we've tried to take that we've had to leave early because of Ellen fucking Lawson. She says 'jump' and you're asking how high before she's even finished talking. You don't care about how much she disrespects our relationship because your head is stuck too far up her backside."

Lisa had no idea what to say. Nora had been upset before, but she had never noticed any of this. She tried to find her words.

"Well...it's not like I do it all the time..."

Nora gave an exasperated cry and turned away.

"Go to your master, Lisa. Your things will be packed and ready to go when you get back."

"What? You're throwing me out?"

"This house is under my name, and I can't stand to look at you right now. If you're going to choose Ellen every time, you should go and live with her. I'm not going to be second-best in my own relationship. God only knows why I put up with it for this long. I must need my head examined." Nora walked towards the house, slamming the driver's door as she went past. "Get out of my sight, Lisa. I'm done."

Lisa watched her go, unsure of what had just happened. Did Nora just break up with her? All because of her friendship with Ellen? Lisa had thought Nora was resentful, but she was actually jealous they had a great bond?

Shaking her head, Lisa shut her door. Nora would calm down eventually. She would get the hissy fit out of her system, and then she would be asking Lisa to come back. The woman couldn't cope without her; it was why she had never left.

She would accept Ellen again, and things would go back to

normal, or as normal as they could with Lisa's friends and colleagues dropping like flies.

She just needed to check on Ellen first and make sure she was okay. Then she would talk it out with Nora once they had calmed down.

A rustling of leaves directly behind her made Lisa jump and she spun around. But there was no one there. It was just the damn fucking wind. Lisa let out a heavy sigh, clutching at her chest. She was jumping at the wind now, all because of this lunatic running around.

Why did she have to come running back into the fire when she had an opportunity to get away for a while?

Because it's Ellen. You would do anything for Ellen.

Her bags were still on the drive, haphazardly left all over the place. Sighing, Lisa went to retrieve them. It wouldn't take long to toss them into her car and then get over to Ellen's. It was just a couple of minutes down the road.

A few hours making sure Ellen was okay and giving Nora space would be enough for both of them to calm down. Then they could talk about everything, and Lisa would be able to get Nora to see her point of view.

As Lisa approached her car, nestled around the side of the house under a tree, pretty much obscured from sight, she noticed that something didn't look right. She couldn't put her finger on it, though. Something was different about the car. It hadn't moved, as far as she could tell.

But it did look a little wonky.

Lisa didn't see it until she was up close. One of her tyres was flat. Dropping her bags, she hurried over. Sure enough, the front nearside tyre was completely flat. Shit, what had happened? It was fine when she had used it to go to town before they left.

But it wasn't just flat. The rubber was ripped. It looked like someone had slashed it to shreds. What the hell?

Then the fluttering of paper caught Lisa's attention. Something was attached to a nearby tree. It looked like a blank piece of paper pinned to the bark, but Lisa could tell that there was something on the other side. Going over to the tree, she managed to unpin it and turned it around.

Jane's picture, smiling up at her. She was sitting on a swing, with a beaming grin and her eyes sparkling. It was the happiest Lisa had ever seen her. But it was the words written underneath that made her go cold despite the warm wind wrapping around her.

You're next.

Lisa gasped when she felt someone grab the back of her head, pulling her off-balance by her hair. Before she knew what was happening, something sharp dug into the skin of her neck and dragged across her throat. Lisa tried to scream, but the pain was too much. Everything came out as a gargle.

Then she was dropped, landing hard on the ground. Lisa clutched at her throat, feeling the blood seeping through her fingers. It felt like her body had gone into shock, clarity slowly setting in.

Someone had just cut her throat.

A movement above her had Lisa looking around. She could barely move her head, but she could see the person standing over her, holding a Stanley knife in a gloved hand.

Lisa couldn't believe it. Was it...this was...

How had she not figured it out?

The picture was picked up off the floor and then it was thrust into her face.

"If you didn't want to die like this, you should have said no. Because of you and the others, people are dead."

"Please..." Lisa croaked. How was she still talking? "I...you..."

"This should have been done years ago. Better late than never." The picture was screwed into a tight ball. "Do me a favour and die quietly. I'm not interested."

Lisa tried to fight, but she could as the paper ball was pushed into her mouth.

Chapter Sixteen

Tuesday 8th May 2001

She finally told her parents. She told them everything when Miss S wouldn't. Did QB's little lapdog think she could explain away how a student ended up getting stabbed through the hand with a Stanley knife in art class? Something that had been purposefully brought out when her back was turned. She said J was just clumsy and stabbed herself when playing around with the knife.

And the head wouldn't call the police. Again.

I told J that enough was enough. She had to tell. She was going to get killed if she didn't tell her parents. They would believe her, and to hell with the repercussions. She would die if this carried on.

I stayed with her when it happened. There was a lot of confusion and anger, and finally J's mum collapsed in hysterics. Her dad was in shock. Neither of them knew what to do for a while. I just held onto J as she sobbed, begging for her parents to take her away, and she can't take it anymore.

It's taken nine months of torture and cover ups, but she's done it. I know I'm not going to have my friend in class anymore, but I'm relieved. I want her to get out of there. J doesn't deserve to be hurt like this because of these bitches.

I wish I could go with her as well. Before, I was mostly left alone because I was considered different. But I stood up for J. I will become a target when they don't have their favourite punching bag.

That's going to change, though. Mum is planning on leaving Dad and taking us away. She thinks that this school is like living in hell. But Dad refuses to leave. He says he has one of the best jobs anyone could ask for, and he won't leave. Even if it means leaving it open for me and my sister to get hurt.

I won't let Leanne become a target. She doesn't deserve that. When Mum leaves Dad, I'm not going to regret it. J will be able to get away, and so will I.

If I never see any of these shits again, I'll be content. But if they come back into my life, I hope I can be strong enough to stop them from doing it again.

* * *

Ellen wiped the steam from the mirror and stared at her reflection. Her hair was hanging wet on her shoulders, her face flushed from the hot water. The dark circles were still there, but she looked better than she had when she first entered the bathroom.

David had suggested having a bath to help relax, but sitting in hot water thinking about what happened and what could happen didn't sound relaxing. So Ellen had had a quick shower instead, scrubbing herself all over until it hurt. It did make her feel a little better, even if her skin was tingling and not in a good way.

She felt a little more human. Maybe she could cope, after all.

She didn't need medication to keep herself in check. She didn't need someone watching over her thinking that she was a danger to herself. Ellen knew how to take care of herself. All she had to do was do plenty of exercise and find natural ways to cleanse herself.

The exercise part was easy enough. Ellen had walked up and down in the garden while David had a meeting in one of the side rooms so he wouldn't be disturbed. It had helped her body to stop feeling like she was walking through treacle. The shower afterwards wiped away the last of her sluggishness.

Although she wished that it would wipe away her cuts and bruises. Her fingers were sore from accidentally punching that metal gate on her walk the day before, and she had a burn on her arm that seemed to have come out of nowhere. She must have put her elbow in some bleach; Jake had cleaned the house, after all. Or maybe she got some on her when she found Kerry's body. That was all she could think of.

And she had managed to get the blood off her neck, although the abrasion on her collarbone was still there. She had scrubbed so hard that she had almost taken a layer of epidermis off. Ellen knew she would have to be careful with her skin at her age; she didn't want to end up withering away because she was vicious to her body. The skin on her thighs were permanently damaged from her ministrations in the past.

Jake hadn't care about it. Nor had Miles. But they're guys. As long as they're getting some, they don't care what a woman looks like.

Ellen leaned on the sink as she felt a flash of regret. She hadn't wanted Jake to leave. He was dependable, and he had always been on her side. Not having him here made Ellen feel very lonely. And Miles...

Even though she used him as just someone to fuck when Jake was too busy to pay attention to her, Ellen had cared for him. He didn't deserve to die like that. None of them did.

Pushing away thoughts of the two men, Ellen dried and dressed, feeling a little wobbly as she tried to push her legs into her jeans. She had to lean against the bath to put her clothes on. Damn, she was still feeling a little woozy. Or she was just lightheaded because of the shower.

If only it would explain her patchy memory. Ellen hated that things came and went, and she would lose chunks of her memory, even if she had just done it. She had seen her mother go through it when she got dementia. Could the same thing be happening to her?

Ellen had no idea. Maybe she should take her husband's advice and go back to the doctor. They had to know why she was losing time. Hopefully, they wouldn't tell her that it was because she was off her medication. Ellen was aware of her condition, but she had it under control. She didn't need drugs to deal with it.

Then again, if it was one of the side-effects of not taking her medication...

Ellen pushed that away. She would not be persuaded to go back on the drugs. They made her feel like shit, anyway.

David was opening the front door as Ellen came down the stairs, and Elizabeth came inside. She said something to David, her hand on his chest. David didn't move it away, giving her a small smile. Then he saw Ellen and pulled away.

"Ellen. How was your shower?"

"I'm feeling a little better now." Ellen gave Elizabeth a smile. "Hey, you."

"Hey." Elizabeth hesitated, and then she approached Ellen and hugged her. "I don't know what to say in this situation."

"Then maybe don't say anything at all." Ellen patted her back before easing Elizabeth away. "It's still pretty raw. I don't think I quite believe it."

"I get that." Elizabeth glanced at David. "Do you want me to stay with her, or are you hanging around as well?"

"I was going to stay, but I just got a call from my landlord. He reminded me to feed the animals, and I've completely forgotten." David grimaced. "I don't want to get into trouble and have my rent raised because I forgot something simple."

Elizabeth looked a little said about that, and Ellen had to fight back a smile. The receptionist's behaviour around their new headteacher was quite cute. She wondered if David was actually going to see it or if he was going to keep it strictly professional. That would certainly be a bright moment in the current darkness.

"Then you go and do that," she said. "Elizabeth and I will be fine."

"If you're sure?"

"I'm sure."

David nodded and picked up his bag by the door, slinging it over his shoulder.

"I might just go and check on Leanne first, see if she's calmed down. I'll try and persuade her to rethink her decision to quit."

"Leanne quit?" Elizabeth frowned. "She said that?"

"She's panicking, which is understandable. Maybe I can change her mind. I've already got to figure out where we're going to get replacements from." David shook his head. "I'm really not looking forward to the start of term now. Everything's gone to shit."

Ellen didn't say anything. She wasn't looking forward to it, either. Things had gone to shit.

"Maybe we can contact all the parents and say school has been delayed and we're doing online teaching for a bit?" she suggested. "These murders are going to be in the news now, so I'm sure everyone will know about them by now."

"I suppose. What about the overseas students?"

"Let's hope we can catch them before they leave," Elizabeth replied. "I can do that for you."

David gave her a smile.

"Thanks, Elizabeth. That would be helpful. We'll talk about that later?"

Elizabeth nodded. Ellen noticed that David's gaze lingered on her for a moment longer before turning away and opening the door.

"I'll be back later. Keep the door locked."

"We will." Ellen approached the door. "We can take care of ourselves."

She watched him walk to his car before shutting the door and putting the chain on, turning the inside lock. Even then, she didn't feel safe. After all, someone had managed to get into Kerry's house and out again, locking up after themselves.

Don't think about that. You're just going to go crazy trying to figure it out.

"You think he'll be okay out there?"

Ellen turned to Elizabeth.

"I doubt he's going to get attacked in broad daylight, Elizabeth."

"Yeah, well, you never know..."

Ellen shook her head and led the way into the kitchen.

"I'm sure David is going to be fine. Once he's done what he needs to do, he'll be back. You don't need to worry about him so much."

Elizabeth didn't answer. She just leaned against the counter, staring at the floor. It had been a while since Ellen had seen the girl so bashful. Maybe this crush on David was deeper than she thought.

They could make a good couple if David got his head out of his backside.

Filling up the kettle and putting it on, Ellen turned to face the other woman.

"I hope the police find who did this. I don't want to be the one to find the next body."

"Next body?" Elizabeth's head shot up. "You think there's going to be another body?"

"With the way things are going, I wouldn't be surprised. I just don't want to be the first person on the scene."

"I don't blame you for that," Elizabeth murmured. Then she straightened up. "Oh, Lisa called. She said that she was on her way back. She'll be here soon."

Ellen frowned.

"What? Lisa's coming back? I thought she and Nora were going to the coast."

"Leanne and David texted everyone about the situation. Lisa immediately came back."

"I'm sure Nora's going to be happy about that."

"From what I heard on the phone, she wasn't. But I'm sure she'll understand." Elizabeth absently twirled a finger through her hair, something she did as a little girl when she was nervous. "Let's hope we can figure out who's crazy enough to kill three people."

"Four," Ellen murmured.

"What? Did you say four?" Elizabeth stared. "Who's the fourth? As far as I know, nobody else has been killed."

Ellen absently scratched the abrasion on her neck, then she stopped abruptly. She was going to end up making it bleed again. Besides, it was making her knuckles hurt. The bruises were quite impressive. Ellen wouldn't be surprised if she had broken something.

Going to the hospital could wait, though.

"Charlie Savedra is dead as well."

Elizabeth's mouth fell open.

"Mr Savedra? How?"

"Fell while walking on Kinder Scout. It's a place in the Peak District," Ellen added when she saw the look of confusion. "It was ruled an accident, but his wife thinks it was suicide."

"And you think it was murder."

It wasn't a question. Ellen nodded.

"Charlie wouldn't go walking out there. He hated it if he could avoid it. I think he was pushed."

"That's a bit of a stretch, isn't it?"

"Possibly. But given everything that's been happening here, I'm more inclined to believe that it's linked."

"Do we know anything more beyond that?"

"Not yet. It's what Leanne and David told me."

Elizabeth fished out her phone and unlocked the screen.

"Okay, give me a few minutes. I'll see what I can find."

"You think you can glean something?"

"Maybe I can find a news article that says something about it. You never know. Maybe there's something we can link to this mess." Elizabeth moved towards the dining room door. "It shouldn't take long."

Ellen was sure Elizabeth could find something. She was very resourceful when she needed to be. It was what made her competent at her job.

And the perfect puppet when the need arose. Those strings had snapped before, but she was easy to manipulate. Just the right amount of coaxing, and Elizabeth was perfect. Hopefully, David wouldn't do that to her; Ellen didn't want her favourite girl other than her daughter to end up in a bad way because of one man.

He had the ability to really break her heart, and he didn't even know it.

A buzzing in her pocket made Ellen jump. She had almost forgotten about her phone. Her heart sank when she saw the name. Why couldn't it be Jake calling her? Why did it have to be this annoying bitch?

Trying to hold back the annoyance, Ellen answered.

"Hi, Nora. I was told..."

"YOU FUCKING LITTLE BITCH!"

Ellen jumped and almost dropped her phone. Her ear was still ringing as she collected herself.

"What the...? Nora, what...?"

"Lisa is dead! DEAD! And it's all because of you! You are going to fucking regret your life, Ellen!"

Chapter Seventeen

The words swirled around her head before slamming into her. Did she just say Lisa was dead?

"What...where...HOW?"

"Someone jumped her in the driveway and slashed her throat before stuffing from fucking paper down her throat. I found her when I came out to do the shopping and saw that her car was still there." Nora sounded like she was hyperventilating. "She...her throat was split wide open. I saw the light disappear in front of me."

Nora let out a wail that made Ellen's head hurt. Her legs were shaking, and she leaned on the counter. Oh, God, not Lisa. Not her as well.

"Have you called the police yet?"

"Of course I've already called them! They're here right now. They got that paper from her mouth and showed it to me." Nora was still breathing heavily. "You know what it was, don't you?"

"No, I don't! Why are you...?"

"That girl who was killed. The Christian girl. It was her. The one you hit with your car."

Now the room was beginning to spin. Ellen sagged to the floor.

"What? I never..."

"For years, nobody knew who actually killed that kid. Although rumours were that it was Lisa, and she wasn't meant to be behind the wheel of a car due to a ban. I did wonder if she was capable of leaving a child to die, but deep down I know she would never do that." Nora swallowed hard. "And I also know that Lisa would do anything to protect you. She was so in love with you that she would protect you from getting arrested. And you know it. If you told her to help you hide a body, you would do it."

Where was she getting this from? Nora wasn't even living in the area when Jane died. How could she know about any of this?

How could she get it spot on?

"Lisa protected you because she was in love with you, and you revelled in it." Nora was snarling now. "Now she's dead. And I'm laying the blame firmly at your door."

"Nora, I didn't..."

"If anyone asks how Lisa died, I'm going to make sure they know you're the one at fault. You might not have sliced her throat open, but you definitely got her in that position. Someone should have put you down years ago."

"Nora!"

But Nora had hung up before Ellen could gather her senses. Rage and confusion mixing together into a knot she couldn't undo, Ellen lowered her phone to the floor. Lisa was dead. Her friend who had been at her side all these years, gone. She was not coming back.

Because of her. Nora was right. If this was about Jane, this was because of her.

"Ellen?"

The voice sounded like she was underwater. It was so far

away. Ellen could see everything moving in front of her, nothing staying still.

This was too much. Way too much.

"Ellen!"

Someone touched her arm, and Ellen flinched, coming back to reality with a thud. Catching herself before she slumped sideways, and looked at the strange yet familiar face beside her. Did she know this person?

Then it all clicked. Of course. Elizabeth. How could she forget her favourite pet?

"Ellen, what happened?" Elizabeth peered at her, her expression showing her concern. "You looked like you'd seen a ghost. I thought you were going to collapse."

Ellen tried to speak, but her mouth had gone dry. She licked her lips.

"Lisa...she's dead."

Elizabeth's eyes widened.

"What? When?"

"Just now. Nora just called me about it."

Her ears were still ringing from Nora screaming at her. Elizabeth looked like she was close to tears herself. She thumped the cabinet beside her.

"Shit! What the hell is going on here? What does this mean?"

"I don't know," Ellen croaked.

Although she had a feeling that with the pool of people involved with Jane's incident getting smaller, she was going to be next. Ellen did not want to get cornered and killed just like them. She took a few deep breaths, trying to bring herself back down. It worked a little bit, but not much. Jake would have been telling her right now that if she had taken her medication, this wouldn't be happening.

Don't even think about Jake right now. Focus on staying alive. Get the upper hand on whoever is doing this.

"What are we going to do now?" Elizabeth asked, chewing on her lower lip. "How do we find out who did this? I don't want to wait around to be killed as well."

"I couldn't agree more." Ellen swallowed hard, trying to get her throat to move. "Get me some wine."

"What? Should you be drinking..."

"Wine! Now!"

Elizabeth flinched, but she got up and went over to the wine rack. Ellen knew she should stick to water, but something stronger was calling her. She felt better after a glass.

And hearing that her closest friend was dead certainly warranted something that wasn't water.

Elizabeth poured a glass of wine with trembling hands, glancing at Ellen as she filled to halfway. Ellen gestured to give her more, and Elizabeth did with a slight hesitation. She filled it almost to the brim, and then carried it over to her. Ellen snatched it away, wine splashing over her hand, and she drank it down in one go, gasping as she lowered the glass. It felt like the wine was sloshing around in her stomach. She closed her eyes and took a few deep breaths.

"Did you find something?"

"What?"

"Charlie Savedra's death. Did you find anything we can use?"

"Oh, right." Elizabeth fumbled for her phone, crouching again beside Ellen. "I found a few articles about the accident, as well as some older news reports about an incident that happened about three years ago."

"What happened?"

"He got charged with stalking and harassment."

Ellen let that sink in. Now that she had not thought Charlie would do. He was too spineless to do something like that.

"Who was he stalking?"

"Bonnie Durose."

"You mean..."

Elizabeth nodded grimly.

"Leanne's older sister had made complaints about him stalking her since he moved to Derbyshire. He was charged, but he didn't get any prison time. Six months later, Bonnie committed suicide."

Ellen remembered what Leanne had said about it. She was still bitter over it all, but she never mentioned Charlie.

"Was there a reason given for why he was harassing her?"

"Apparently, Charlie said through his solicitor that he only wanted to say sorry for what happened when she was a girl. When she was abused at school at the time he was the head-teacher." Elizabeth swallowed. "Not long after Bonnie died, Charlie was dead. Speculation was put forward that he was losing everything because of his actions, or maybe he felt guilty about what happened to Bonnie."

"Bonnie's not the only one, so why was he fixated on her?"

"Apparently, he was trying to get on her mother's good side and have an affair with her, but she told him to pound sand. There's an article over how Charlie and Bonnie crossed paths again because of that and Bonnie's mental health went downhill."

So Charlie had thought it was a good idea to pursue the mother romantically, and when that didn't work, he tried to use Bonnie as a way to get to her. And it had backfired.

Leanne had never mentioned any of this before. She hadn't said a word about meeting Charlie after they left the school.

Maybe she didn't meet him. That could be part of it.

Or perhaps...

"Leanne said she had been at a school in Derbyshire before she came here, yes?"

Elizabeth's eyes widened.

"Yes. I remember that. She said she practically lived in the Peak District."

"Do you remember which school?"

"Edale Primary School. I remember the odd name."

Ellen could feel her pulse quickening. Was this what they were looking for?

"Check how far away Edale is from Kinder Scout."

Elizabeth's gaze went back to her phone as her thumbs moved quickly across the screen, bringing up the maps. Ellen watched as her face changed, staring at the results.

"It's a little over three miles. Practically around the corner." She looked up. "Leanne would still be at the school when Charlie died. She applied for Wolsey Prep not long after."

Now that was definitely not a coincidence. Ellen could see everything fall into place. It was Leanne. The bouncy, bright girl with the ready smile and lighthearted attitude was the one who had done all of this.

They had been working with a lunatic all this time, and nobody had been any the wiser.

Ellen grabbed onto the counter and scrambled to her feet, nearly losing her grip as she hauled herself up.

"We have to call the police."

"What?"

"It's Leanne. She's been killing everyone." Ellen leaned against the sink, trying not to bring up what little there was in her stomach. "Call the police, Elizabeth. They have to arrest her. If they're lucky, they will more than likely catch her disposing of the evidence."

Her expression as horrified as Ellen felt, Elizabeth turned away, stabbing at her phone until she managed to press the buttons she wanted. As she put it to her ear, Ellen went into the hall and pulled on her trainers. Then she snatched up her bag, checking the contents as she slung it over her shoulder.

The Stanley knife was there, nestled next to her hairbrush. Ellen kept it in her bag, just in case. It was also a good defence tool if she needed it. That would be enough to keep the bitch in one place until the police got there.

"Ellen! Where are you going?"

Ellen ignored the shouting, undoing the door and flinging it open. Elizabeth was still shouting, but the words faded as Ellen broke into a run.

* * *

It didn't take long to get to Leanne's house, but Ellen's lungs were burning. She stumbled, nearly falling to her hands and knees in the road. But she got up and carried on, rage building on the adrenaline.

Leanne thought she was so clever. She had come here to kill them, lying in wait until she found a moment to go after them. She had been stalking them the whole time.

This hadn't been about Jane at all. It was about Bonnie. Jane had simply been a smokescreen. They had been thinking about this in the wrong way.

Not anymore. Ellen was going to make sure Leanne paid for what she did.

Leanne's house was a little bit off the road, one of many in a tiny cul-de-sac that backed onto the fields. If you went in almost a straight line, you would reach Lisa's house in a little over a mile. Leanne was a runner. It wouldn't take much to run over, kill Lisa and come back again. She had been on a run as well at the time Kerry had been murdered. Did she even take sips out of that water bottle, or was it all for show?

Thank God she hadn't asked for a drink at the time.

David's car was in the driveway beside Leanne's car. He was coming out as Ellen reached the house, Leanne just behind him. She saw Ellen first, and she froze. David turned, his expression bewildered.

"Ellen? What are you...?"

"Get away from her, David." Ellen was breathing heavily, trying to get air back into her lungs. "She killed them."

"What? What are you...?"

"She's killed them all. Isabella, Miles, Kerry, Lisa. Even Charlie. She's killed all over them."

David stared. Leanne's mouth fell open.

"What the...? What are you talking about, Ellen? I haven't killed anyone."

"Don't lie to me, you stupid little bitch!" Ellen fumbled with her bag, burrowing her hand deep inside. "I know you are the one who murdered everyone. You wanted revenge for what happened to Bonnie twenty years ago. You waited until you were in a position of trust, and then you came after us. Well, I won't let that happen! Not with me!"

She drew out the Stanley knife and flicked out the blade. Leanne gasped, and David jumped in front of her. He held up his hands.

"Ellen, put the knife down."

"She's a killer, David! She needs to face justice!"

"And threatening her with a knife is going to get that, is it?" Ellen barked out a laugh.

"She's murdered five people already. She's not going to stop until someone puts her down." She could feel everything swaying. "Get out of the way, David. I don't want to hurt you."

"Ellen, have you been drinking?"

"She's off her medication," Leanne said, touching David's shoulder. "I think she's hallucinating."

"No!" Ellen screamed. "I'm not hallucinating. Elizabeth was with me when I found out your family interacted with Charlie before his death. You lived near where he died. I know I'm not making it up."

Leanne swallowed.

"But I wasn't anywhere near when he died. I was out of the country."

"Don't lie to me! You can do better than that!"

"It's true. I was taking a sabbatical. George and I were in Ireland."

That sounded so stupid that Ellen couldn't help but giggle.

"You're a good liar, Leanne. I'll give you that. But you're not good enough. I'm going to make sure you know how it feels to have your throat slashed open. You're going to regret messing with me!"

"Ellen!"

Ellen screamed when she felt a hand clamp onto her arm. She threw her weight into the hard body and released herself, slashing with the knife. There was a gasp of pain, and then Ellen was slammed into so hard that her skull rattled. The wind was knocked out of her as she was thrown onto the floor, her bag hitting her in the face before it bounced away, the contents scattering across the drive.

"Leanne, get the knife! Ellen, let go!"

Ellen resisted, trying to yank her arm away as David kept her knife hand in an arm lock. Then Leanne was there, prying Ellen's fingers off the Stanley knife and backing away with the weapon.

"No! No, don't do that!" Ellen panicked. "Help! Someone help me! She's going to kill me!"

"Ellen, calm down!" David struggled against her. "You're going to hurt yourself. Just calm down."

"Let me go, David! Please, she's going to kill us!"

"She's not going to kill anyone. So stop this lunacy!"

Ellen snarled.

"I'm not a lunatic!"

"Did she cut you, David?" Leanne asked. She was staring at the Stanley knife. "You're not bleeding, are you?"

"She cut my t-shirt, but I think she missed me." David didn't let go of Ellen. "Why?"

"Because there's blood on the knife." Leanne's expression was one of shock as she held it out, being careful what she touched. "It doesn't look dry, and there's a fingerprint in it."

Ellen stared at it. That hadn't been there before.

"That...that's not mine!" She protested.

"It's the one I took out of your hand, Ellen. It's yours." Leanne put it carefully on the porch step. "I'm going to call the police."

"Hurry back out," David said gruffly. "I'm going to need help restraining Ellen."

Restraining her? No, not again. Ellen couldn't go through with that. She bucked, but David wouldn't budge.

"David, please! No!" She began to sob. "You've got it all wrong. It was her!"

208

"We need to wait for the police, Ellen." David's voice was grim. "We're going to let them deal with this. You just need to calm down."

"I can't do that! Leanne is going to get away if we don't get her! She's going to get away with it!"

David shook his head.

"Jake warned me that your hallucinations and memory loss had been getting worse lately. I told him I trusted your judgement. Now I regret doing that. I should have listened to him."

What was he saying? He didn't believe her. Ellen couldn't get this to sink in. David said he thought she was insane. He believed what her husband had said.

She hadn't killed anyone. The police would find that out. This would work out eventually.

Then she would make sure the bitch got her just desserts.

Chapter Eighteen

Two Weeks Later

Elizabeth pulled up outside David's house. His car was there, so he was home. Or somewhere around if he was helping the farmer. That was how he spent his Sundays, apparently, helping the farmer and his wife with their land when he was supposed to be resting.

Then again, given what had happened two weeks ago, it was no surprise that he was trying to find something to take his mind off the fact they had been in close quarters with a killer.

When Elizabeth had heard that Ellen was the one who had killed everyone, she hadn't quite believed it. Ellen was a vicious bitch when she wanted to be, but she used her words to get her point across. The only time she had killed someone was when she ran Jane over, and that she had confessed to after having a nervous breakdown during her police interview. Talking about it for the first time seemed to have broken something in her.

At least she hadn't said what had happened beforehand, or after. Otherwise more than Ellen would be in serious trouble.

But she refused to acknowledge the other murders, although the evidence was pointing to her: there were her prints on everything at Miles' murder, a chemical burn on her arm and a bruised hand from where she broke Kerry's nose, not to mention Lisa's blood on her Stanley knife. Plus they had found a pay-as-you-go phone that she had used to lure Miles to his death in her bag. At some point, she had switched it with her original number.

Ellen kept denying it. She kept screaming that she wouldn't do that, but her memory gaps and the time she was away from the house at the time of each murder could not be accounted for. It just made her more suspicious.

Elizabeth felt awful for her. They had been friends for a long time, and Elizabeth had looked up to her. But she was also relieved that Ellen had been caught before Elizabeth was killed as well.

She shuddered to think what Ellen might have had planned for her. At least she was on a mental health ward after attempting suicide in her cell. She would always have someone watching her.

After a little searching, Elizabeth found David in the farmyard. He was leaning on the fence around the pigsty, watching as the pigs slumbered fitfully at the far side, keeping under their shelter to avoid the hot sun. It was September now, and it felt like an Indian summer. David was wearing a pair of shorts and trainers, but no shirt. Elizabeth could see the sweat glistening on his back, and she wanted to run her hands over his body.

Shoving her hands into her pockets, she approached him. David looked over his shoulder, giving her a slight smile.

"Hey."

"Hey." Elizabeth paused. God, she wished she would stop losing her confidence around him. She was not sixteen anymore. "What are you doing out here? It's not Sunday."

"I was just checking on the animals. The farmer asked if I

could feed them."

"Is he not here?"

David shook his head.

"Their daughter is getting married in Lincoln. He and the missus have gone for the weekend. I said I would look after things while they were away."

"Oh. I see." Hesitating for just a moment, Elizabeth joined him at the fence. "It feels odd that we're teaching the kids online right now. It's like we're back in the pandemic."

"Yeah, that was rough. But it's only temporary. We're going to be fine." David shrugged. "Sometimes, we have to adjust when we don't like it, but it works out. Wolsey Prep will be back to normal soon."

"Normal. I don't think it will be again." Elizabeth leaned on the fence, trying to ignore the stench coming from the pigs. "Four teachers have been murdered in as many days, and a fifth is on a psych ward. The school's reputation is going to go downhill."

"It's already gone downhill. The board has been talking to me about it." David took a deep breath. "They've decided to have a new headteacher come in and start the place from scratch."

Elizabeth stared. This was the first she was hearing about it.

"What? You were fired?"

"No, I was offered to stay on in my position as English teacher, but I just can't." David straightened up, rubbing a hand across his bare chest. "I'll take a sabbatical, and then I'll start up elsewhere. That should give me enough time to get over what happened here."

Elizabeth couldn't believe what he was saying. He was going to leave? If he did that, she would never see him again.

"You can't go!" she blurted out.

"Oh?" David arched an eyebrow. "Why not?"

"You can't! I don't want you to go!"

"I'm sure you can manage without me, Elizabeth."

But Elizabeth shook her head.

"No, I won't." She reached for him, touching his chest with both hands. Muscles tensed under her palms, and she almost got distracted. Elizabeth cupped his cheeks. "If you do go, take me with you. I don't want to be here without you."

"Elizabeth..."

"I'm in love with you, David. I've been trying to fight it for a long time, but I can't have you leave without me saying it. And I want to be with you. Take me with you when you go. Please."

Not exactly the romantic way Elizabeth wanted to do it, but she couldn't stop herself. She rose up on tiptoe and kissed him. David didn't move, although his hands went to her waist. But that was it. He didn't kiss her back.

Embarrassment taking over, Elizabeth pulled back, lowering her hands.

"I...I thought..."

"You're a beautiful woman, Elizabeth. If I didn't know what a nasty piece of work you were, I would have taken you to bed a long time ago."

"What?" Elizabeth blinked. "What did you say?"

"You want to know why I would never have anything to do with someone like you?" David's expression hardened, his eyes darkening. He looked like a different man. "Because you killed my sister."

Sister? What was he...?

Elizabeth gurgled as David's hands went around her neck and began to squeeze. David shook his head.

"You didn't think you would get out of this unscathed, did

you, Elizabeth? I saved you for last."

* * *

When Elizabeth came round, she found that she was lying on the ground. And it was soft, sticky and smelly. Very smelly. Blinking her eyes open, her throat burning, she took stock of her surroundings.

Then she realised that she was tied up. Her ankles were bound together with rope, as were her wrists, firmly secure behind her back. She could wriggle and move a little, but that was it.

What the hell just happened? Where was she? Looking around, she could see that she was in the corner of the pigsty, tucked out of sight of the main yard. The pigs were being kept away from her by a closed gate, but they were snorting loudly and looking at her through the gaps in the fence.

Also, what the hell was that smell? It wasn't the mud or the stench from the animals. It was something else, and it seemed to be coming from her. What had she been rolled in?

Then Elizabeth remembered what had happened before her memory stopped. She had been with David. He said she killed his sister, and then...

What he said stuck in her head. David was related to...Jane? That was the only link she could find. But how had she not made the connection? He was too old to be the younger brother.

But Jane had an older brother. He was in university at the time. And you met him.

And I didn't make the connection between then and now.

"I'm surprised you didn't recognise me, if I'm honest."

Elizabeth gasped and rolled over, only to moan as her hands got squashed under her back. She adjusted herself and looked up at David, who was leaning over the stone wall. He gave her a smirk that looked cold.

"When I saw you sitting behind the desk the day I came in for the first time, I recognised you immediately. But you didn't seem to know who I was. I was surprised, given that you had seen me when I visited my parents, and you had declared that I was pretty fit. I suppose if I had my stepfather's name, you might have clicked who I was."

"I remember you now," Elizabeth croaked.

God, it hurt to talk. And her heart was pounding against her ribcage. She felt sick. What was he going to do to her? Elizabeth tried not to hyperventilate.

"It was you? You killed them all?"

David tilted his head to one side, regarding her with an expression that made Elizabeth want to run away. She would have done it if she was unbound.

"If I'd known about this years ago, I would have done this long before now." David's voice was calm, not like what she was used to. He hopped up onto the wall and sat with his legs crossed. His chest was now covered by a simple blue polo shirt, stretched across his biceps. "But I only knew what Jane had told Mum and Dad. It wasn't much, but it was enough for them to file a civil suit against Ellen Lawson and her friends. After all, she was the ringleader. She believed that her position had been usurped because Mum took over the hockey teams, something she believed was her domain. So that's why she decided to go after Jane. Such a pathetic reason for a pathetic woman.

"But she never laid a hand on Jane. She didn't need to when she had you, a London girl who had been expelled from three schools before you came to Wolsey Prep for violence. Impressive when you're only in primary school. But your parents are decent people, so I shudder to think that you were born to be a violent and mean little bitch."

"It's not what you think," Elizabeth protested. She struggled to sit up, feeling her stomach muscles strain as they took the weight. "I was manipulated into it by Ellen as well. She was the driving force behind it all, and I was too scared to go against her."

"So you didn't report this to another teacher? You didn't tell anyone what you were up to?"

"There were several teachers involved! I didn't know who to trust."

David shook his head.

"If I hadn't read about all of the details that happened while Jane was here, then I might have believed you. After all, you were a kid as well. But what I read made me realise you were just as complicit, and just as disgusting as Ellen Lawson and her group of lackeys."

"Read about what?"

"You didn't know? Jane kept a diary. She wrote down everything that happened to her, including the conversations she overheard you having with the various teachers involved in this pathetic campaign. You were in this just as much as they were, and you were enjoying the fact you could physically and mentally torment someone smaller than you and get away with it."

Jane had kept a diary? Elizabeth had never seen that. Bonnie was the one constantly scribbling in a book, but Jane must have done it as well. She did keep to herself, and she liked to read for the most part. Had she kept a diary as well?

God, if she had known, she would have found the damn thing and ripped it to shreds.

"How we didn't find it when we were clearing out Jane's things twenty years ago, I have no idea. Mum had just packed all of her belongings into boxes and put them in the attic. She couldn't bring herself to donate any of it. I was looking around for something a couple of years ago, and I came upon the diary. You can imagine how shocked I was when I read what happened. Mum and Dad had no idea it existed." David scowled. "To think you targeted her just because Ellen Lawson had a hissy fit."

"It wasn't meant to go that far," Elizabeth whispered. She could feel the tears building and clogging her already sore throat. How had she gotten into this situation? "We were just meant to let Jane know where her place was."

That was clearly the wrong thing to say because David jumped off the wall and kicked her in the stomach. Elizabeth was knocked onto her back, pain coming from her stomach and her hands. She rolled onto her side, trying to gasp in air.

"She was twelve years old!" David bellowed. "Twelve! She did nothing wrong except have parents Ellen had a grievance with. Instead of talking it out like proper adults, she decided to be a bitch and target the daughter. And I thought this sort of mentality stopped when we're in secondary school. She was a fucking grown up! Besides, you tried to drown her, threw hot glue and acid on her, and you took every opportunity to hit her and make it look like an accident. How can you justify that as letting Jane know her place? That's just a cop out."

Elizabeth felt sick. She could feel her stomach threatening to empty its contents, the bile building in her throat. David crouched before her and grabbed her head by the hair. Elizabeth moaned as she was yanked up, the pain in her head overtaking the nausea.

"They were all there when you led the attack on my little

sister," David hissed into her face. "She did nothing wrong. She begged you to stop, begged for help. And nobody did anything. Everyone closed ranks when the police were involved, and they couldn't do anything. Jane had to suffer because a grown woman threw her toys out of the fucking pram."

Elizabeth couldn't answer. If she did, she was more than likely going to be sick. Although she did contemplate aiming it at David, hoping that he would let her go.

"None of those pieces of shits did anything. And Ellen Lawson...she thought she could do whatever she wanted. To the point that she would run a twelve-year-old girl over after you pushed her in front of the car."

"No," Elizabeth croaked.

David growled and thrust her away from him. Elizabeth went down like a sack of potatoes, jarring her shoulder on the floor. He stood up and paced away.

"You were witnessed by Bonnie Durose. She saw what you did, and you know she saw the whole thing! You threatened her about telling anyone about what happened, saying that you would come after her if she said a word about it to anyone. You scared her so much that she was silent about it for twenty years. Nobody knew what happened, and she was so torn up with guilt over not being able to say anything for fear of you or the others coming after her that she turned to drugs. It was the only way she could cope with what she saw. No matter how bad it got, Bonnie wouldn't say a word. You really terrified her."

"But...how do you know?" Elizabeth licked her dry lips. "Did Leanne tell you? I saw her watching us when I talked to Bonnie that day."

"So you're admitting that you threatened Bonnie?" David barked out a laugh. "I shouldn't be surprised by now. No,

Bonnie and I were at the same running club for a while. We actually didn't live too far from each other. Who knew that our families would end up in the same part of the world after such a tragedy? She left me a letter before she died, saying she didn't want to die without clearing her conscience, and she couldn't forgive herself for not saying a word. I can't be angry at her for being another victim."

So Bonnie had tattled. Elizabeth gritted her teeth. If she was alive and Elizabeth wasn't tied up like an animal, she would have made sure Bonnie knew she had done the wrong thing.

She would not go to prison.

"What are you going to do when the police find out that Ellen was framed?" she asked. "They're going to come looking again."

"Oh, but they won't. I've made sure that there's no room for error." David smirked. "Besides, Ellen is diagnosed as bipolar with a personality disorder, not to mention a schizoaffective disorder. That's a combination that makes her a dangerous individual if she's not under control. Her husband's already told the doctors and the police that she's been suffering from delusions for years. They'll see what happened as a psychotic break, especially with her off her medications. She got it into her head that she was avenging Jane for what happened, so she went after those who failed her, forgetting the fact that she was the ringleader."

It sounded so easy, and yet...

"Do you really think that will stand up in court?"

"She'll either go to jail or she'll be kept permanently in the mental health ward. As long as she goes through the psychological hell she put my sister through, I don't care where she goes."

He sounded so cold. Elizabeth was stunned that she had once had feelings for him. They were gone now, and she was left feeling like she had been cheated. David had led her on, and he had done it so effortlessly.

She used an elbow to push herself upright.

"You do realise that if I turn up dead now then the police are going to know that Ellen didn't kill me. They'll start looking again."

"Nope. They won't."

"How can you be so confident?"

David chuckled.

"Come on, think about it. Ellen can't have carried a body from the river to the house on her own or overpowered a grown man. She's not that strong. The police know that she had to have help. Which was why I planted evidence that you were part of it as well."

"*What?*"

"It's been known for a long time that you're Ellen's little lapdog. You do what she wants. Of course you would help her with a few murders if she asked you. You're worse than Lisa when Ellen clicks her fingers. She hasn't mentioned your name yet, but it doesn't matter. Your DNA was found at Kerry's house and on Miles' body." David took off his glasses and cleaned them on the hem of his shirt. "I had a call from the police a while ago, asking about you and what you were like. I answered them honestly, of course, but there is a warrant out for your arrest."

Elizabeth felt like she was in a nightmare. This couldn't be happening. How had she ended up in this situation?

That stupid bitch shouldn't have opened her mouth. And to Jane's brother, of all people. Who knew he was a psychopath?

"I'll tell them everything," she hissed, glaring up at him. "I'll make sure the police know the truth."

"I knew you would say that. You don't go down without a fight. I have to admire that, even though I despise you." David put his glasses back on. "Which is why I'm going to make it look like you've disappeared without a trace. A few clues here and there will suggest that you took off out of the country. Nobody will be able to find you."

"How are you going to do that?"

"Elizabeth, I know you're a disgusting human being, but you do have a brain." David gestured at their surroundings. "Look where we are. Haven't you seen the movie *Hannibal*?"

Elizabeth's heart stuttered. She had seen that movie. It was one she had snuck into because she wasn't old enough to watch it. She remembered the scene with the pigs and how they tore the bad guy apart. That had left her with nightmares for a while.

Oh, God. He wasn't...

"Bonnie called you PB. Princess Bitch. That sounded very appropriate to me." David wandered over to the gate, where the pigs were trying to get in by bumping up against the fence. "My sister called you LMP. Little Miss Piggy. You had a diva attitude all the time and a violent nature. And she said you were about as ugly as a pig."

LMP? Elizabeth remembered the anonymous letter she received with her police record. She stared at David. That had been him?

Why was she so surprised now?

"Seeing as you were known as a pig, I thought being smeared in truffles and devoured by pigs would be very appropriate." David leaned on the gate as he watched her. "Less for me to clean up."

Now Elizabeth really felt sick. She contemplated screaming, but the farm was far away from everyone else, and the only people who lived on the actual farm weren't around.

They were alone.

"How are you going to get domesticated pigs to eat me? They're not going to do that."

"You don't think you stink a bit? I smeared you with the scent of truffles. And pigs go foraging for truffles, whether they are domesticated or not." David gestured at the animals. The snorting seemed to have gotten louder. "Also, I haven't actually fed them all the while their owners have been away. So they're very hungry. And when domesticated pigs are hungry, they'll eat anything. Including humans."

He was serious? Elizabeth's panic left her frozen as she watched David climb onto the stone wall, one hand on the latch of the gate.

"I'd like to say it's been a pleasure, Elizabeth, but that would be a lie. I did enjoy teasing you and have you thinking I was interested. You did know how to flatter me. But after what you did to my sister, and how you have no remorse for what you committed, I can't let you walk away." He undid the gate and stood up. "Enjoy getting up close and personal with those you're closely associated with. I'm sure it's going to be a scream."

Elizabeth watched as the pigs pushed open the gate with their snouts and wandered into the area. She wanted to get up and run away, but she couldn't move. David had tied her up really tightly. Her heart was in her mouth as one pig sniffed the air and prowled closer to her. She could see the glint in its eye. It could smell the truffles. If David was right about them being starving, it wouldn't be long until they realised where the smell was coming from.

And David just stood there, arms folded and watching her with a smug look, a cold gleam in his eyes. It was like the man she had fallen for was gone and there was a complete stranger in front of her.

A stranger who was revelling in the fact he was going to watch her die.

One of the pigs started sniffing at her face. Elizabeth scrambled backwards, her shoulder hitting the wall. She tried to get up, only to free when the pig came closer and sniffed her face. Its breath was awful, and it made her want to gag.

Please let this be a dream. Please.

But when she felt teeth sink into her calf from a second pig, Elizabeth knew this was not a dream she would be waking up from.

And, despite a pig's snout with teeth showing so close to her face, she screamed.

Chapter Nineteen

Saturday 19th May 2000

She was supposed to be gone. But not like this.

I heard the scream from my room. Then the bang. From my window I saw a car by the changing rooms. It looked familiar, and I saw QB getting out and looking freaked. She looked like she knew she was in trouble. I thought she had hit another car.

Then I saw PB. She looked like she was going to faint. QB is telling her to stop being such a baby, and nobody is going to know. They can get through this. At the time, I didn't know what she meant.

Miss S joins them, and she's just as distraught. She started screaming at PB about how she had gone too far, but QB tells her to shut up and help her take the car away. As soon as she orders her to do that, Miss S does it. Like she always does.

When they left, I went outside to look. And I found J. She was in a crumbled mess on the ground, her eyes open and staring at me. I've never felt so cold in my life.

I've never seen a dead body before.

There are adults around. The athletics tournament is still going on. And somehow there was no one around to see what happened.

I have to get help. But if I tell, they are going to know it was me. I'm the only one who's stood up to them. When J isn't around, they go after me because it's fun. If I tell anyone what I actually saw, they're going to make it worse for me. Even if Mum believes me, there's nothing we can do. They'll make sure it goes away and doesn't exist anymore.

QB knows how to make everything go away if it's not to her narrative. Miss S will always be her lapdog. And PB will never be punished. She's just as disgusting as the queen bitch.

I'm so sorry J. I wish things could have gone better. And I wish I was strong enough to fight for you.

* * *

The screams had stopped a while ago. David sat in his kitchen and sipped his coffee. It had been both satisfying to hear and uncomfortable, mostly due to the sound Elizabeth was making. That had been a horrible noise.

But it wasn't less than what she deserved. She was destined to be ripped to shreds. While doing it mentally and publicly would have worked, having it done physically was even better.

And there was no chance of her arguing back and getting anyone to listen to her. David was so fed up with hearing her voice.

There wouldn't be much left of her once the pigs were done. It was amazing what they could eat when they were starving. All David had to do was clean up the remains and feed the pigs properly, and nobody would be any the wiser.

He wasn't quite done, but it was almost over, thank God. David was exhausted from it all. Murder was not something to be taken lightly, and some people might think he had taken it too far. A part of him would agree with them. This was not something David normally did.

But anything else would have been too good for those who had been a part of his sister's bullying and demise. They had stood by and let all of it happen.

As for Ellen Lawson, making it look like she had murdered everyone had felt appropriate for her. When Jake had told David in confidence that his wife had a schizoaffective disorder in reference to understanding David's false story about having a sister struggling with depression, he had provided vital information. Jake would have, inadvertently, been the reason for Ellen's demise.

Having her locked up due to her mental instability, knowing that she was innocent but nobody would believe her, sounded just about right for her. Although David would have liked to have picked her apart before killing her. That would have made him feel just as good.

But maybe that was a bit too much, even for him. He had done enough.

A knock at the door had David looking up. Putting his coffee mug down, he stood up and went into the living room. Leanne was in the doorway, wearing baggy jeans and a simple yellow blouse. Her hair looked freshly washed and was pinned back from her face. She gave him a smile.

"Hey."

"Hey." David looked over her. "You certainly would pass for Elizabeth at a distance."

"In the dark and from the back, it should be perfect."

"You know what you're going to do?"

Leanne nodded.

"Drive the car back, get the necessary stuff into a suitcase, drive away and park the car at the airport. The ticket has been booked, and I've managed to find her passport. It will look like she's fled the country. I'll get on the plane and head over to Germany, and then I'll take the train back. The fake passport is good to go for that. Nobody will be able to connect me with it. They'll think I'm with my family on holiday, as I said I would be."

"Good."

Leanne glanced towards the window.

"Is it done now?"

"It's done."

There was a moment's hesitation, and then Leanne strode towards him. David didn't even hesitate as he hugged her, feeling Leanne let out a shuddering breath as she leaned her head on his shoulder. It was like all of the tension had left her body.

"Thank God this is over."

"I concur." David eased Leanne back, hands on her shoulders as he looked at her. "Are you ready to go?"

"Yes. Mum called me and said George is fine at his new school. He's looking forward to seeing me, and I'll be glad to leave this hellhole." Leanne met his gaze. "What about you? When are you leaving?"

"I have to finish off this term, and then I'm off at Christmas. I'd leave sooner, but they need that time to find a replacement for me."

"I thought they managed to replace everyone at the school already."

"I'm not about to argue. I don't want my departure to look suspicious." David shrugged. "With more eyes on me, I've got to be careful."

"Fair enough. Are you going to move back near your parents? I'm sure we can meet up when you're away from here."

227

"I plan to, and I'd like that." David tapped Leanne's chin with his finger. "We make a pretty good team, don't we? Almost like we were made to be partners."

Leanne's eyes glinted. She sighed.

"When I came here, I was planning on trying to find something to blackmail Ellen with. Anything to humiliate her. When I found out she was cheating with Miles, I thought I found the goldmine. I took so many pictures that I was spoiled for choice which ones to give Jake. And then you came looking to humiliate her as well."

"I knew she had paid up for the lawsuit, but she still refused responsibility. I wanted answers."

And it was like two kindred spirits coming together. They had found out who the other was, and Leanne had given her sister's diary to David. The contents had been shocking, and David had been shaking with rage once he had finished. To think there were so many sick individuals in one place that wasn't a prison was shocking.

Planning to kill them hadn't been the original scheme. But once Leanne expressed wanting to kill Elizabeth for tormenting both of their sisters, things had taken shape from there.

It wasn't something David would do again, but he was glad he had done it.

The lawsuit settlement wasn't enough. This was what they deserved.

"Just so you know, on the off-chance that Elizabeth survived..." David paused. "I made sure never to mention you. I said Jane wrote the diary, that Bonnie wrote me a letter before she died. If there's a slight chance they figure out that it's me, I'll cover for you. You have my word."

"I know." Leanne touched his chest. "You're sweet when

you want to be, David. I wish I had a big brother like you."

"And I wish I had my sister back. Maybe we can do something about it?"

"I'd like that." Leanne moved on closer and kissed his cheek. "Thank you. I appreciate you helping me. I don't think I could have done it on my own."

"I was going to say the same." David hugged her again. "It's going to be a while before we can meet again, but I'll look forward to it. We won't be living that far away from each other, after all."

"Same here. George will like to see you as well."

"Let him know I'll see him soon. Just let everything die down for now."

"Of course." Leanne wrinkled her nose. "At least you won't have a house stinking of manure."

David laughed.

"That will be a plus. Although I will miss the house in general." He moved towards the kitchen. "I was about to make lunch. How does risotto sound?"

"Sounds awesome. I'm starving." Leanne followed him. "I've got time to kill before it gets dark, and I can't go home on an empty stomach."

"Then I'll make sure you are properly fed." David winked at her. "Want to get the chicken and vegetables out? I'll get the risotto started on the hob."

"Okay." Leanne went to the fridge and opened it. "You know, I don't want to make this a habit. It's not something I could do on a regular basis."

David waited. He could tell Leanne wanted to say more.

"But I can honestly say this," she shot him a grin, "doing what we did was rather therapeutic. That's how I felt after I pushed Charlie Savedra off Kinder Scout when I confronted him for harassing my family. He brought back so many bad memories, and I wanted him gone. Pushing him to his death was certainly a good way to feel better."

David couldn't agree more. He had been feeling that way when he finally took the lives of Isabella and Miles, watching Elizabeth get ripped to pieces by pigs. He saw it when Leanne poured the acid into Kerry's mouth and when she talked about cutting Lisa's throat. It was like a weight was lifted off their shoulders.

It wasn't something either of them were going to make a habit. But it worked for the time they did it.

Just never again. This was enough.